MW01126126

Never

JOY AVERY

NEVER

Copyright© 2017 by Joy Avery

ALL RIGHTS RESERVED

No parts of this book may be reproduced, scanned, or distributed in any printed or electronic form without permission, except for brief quotes used for the purpose of review or promotion. Any trademarks, service marks, or product names are the property of their respective owners, and are used only for reference.

NEVER is a work of fiction. Names, characters, places and incidents are the product of the author's imaginations or used fictitiously. Any resemblance to actual events, locales, or persons, living or dead, is purely coincidental.

ISBN-13: 978-1977675828
ISBN-10: 1977675824

First Print Edition: October 2017

DEDICATION

Dedicated to the dream.

ALSO BY JOY AVERY

Smoke in the Citi
His Until Sunrise
Cupid's Error-a novella
His Ultimate Desire
One Delight Night
A Gentleman's Agreement
Another Man's Treasure
Maybe (a Lassiter Sisters novella-Book 2)
In the Market for Love (Harlequin Kimani Romance)

ACKNOWLEDGMENTS

My thanks—first and foremost—to God for blessing me with this gift of storytelling.

My endless gratitude to my husband and daughter for your unwavering support and patience. I love you both very much!

A huge thank you to my awesome critique partner, Lyla Dune.

To my friends and family who've offered tons and tons of encouragement and support, I express my greatest gratitude. Your support means the world to me.

Chapter 1

Gadiya Lassiter knew fiddling in her purse while driving was a dangerous combination, especially along this lonely stretch of Mount Pleasance, North Carolina. A deer, bear, coyote, or any other number of creatures were liable to dart out in front of her.

But she'd been waiting for correspondence from the Mount Pleasance Fire Department all week and hoped the notification chime she'd just heard was it. She thumbed through the email messages, dividing her focus between the Smartphone screen and the road ahead.

"Finally!" She felt like a giddy five-year-old who'd just received a new pony, instead of the thirty-year-old business woman she actually was. But jovial attitude dimmed quickly reading the message.

Further action is needed by the fire chief?

"Fire chief? What fire chief? We don't have a freaking fire chief."

Mount Pleasance hadn't had a fire chief in over three months, after the last was caught in a compromising position with a married woman. Gadiya had been dealing with the *acting* fire chief. Acting was all he was doing, because he sure as hell didn't know what was going on.

How hard was it to get an answer from the city council?

Ugh.

The man had all but promised her the contract that would allow her balloon art and kids' entertainment company, The Twisted Balloon, to be a part of the upcoming Fireman's Day celebration was a done deal. Although it wasn't until October—four months away—she needed the final word so that she could start ordering the items she'd need.

Maybe she should go directly to the city council herself. No, they'd never approve it without the backing of MPFD, which was the most ridiculous thing she'd ever heard.

Well, no use crying over it now. Gadiya tossed the phone onto the passenger seat. Her eyes slid back to the road just in time to see a figure dart out of the way, hit the ground, and roll several times. She squealed and slammed on the brakes. The convertible Mustang came to a screeching halt, kicking up a cloud of white smoke.

The rancid smell of burning rubber invaded her

nostrils. Blood *whooshed* in her ears.

"*Oh shit, oh shit, oh shit.*"

Gathering her nerves, she fumbled with the seatbelt, her trembling fingers finally managing to unfasten the device.

Her heart slapped against her ribcage as her slick hands gripped at the door handle. She half-stepped, half-fell from the vehicle.

When the figure didn't reemerge, she panicked. "Please let 'em be okay. Please let 'em be okay." All she needed was a vehicular manslaughter charge on her already fragile driving record. She cautiously approached the patch of dried brush.

Nothing.

Her stomach churned as she scanned the weeded area. "H-hello? Are you okay?"

A faint moan slash groan came from deeper in the brush. The mutter was a good sign, right? At least it meant he or she was still alive...for now. Nausea washed over her. Rushing toward the tortured sound, she mentally prepared herself for whatever horrific scene awaited her.

Gadiya breathed a sigh of relief when her eyes landed on a masculine form, sitting upright dusting the red clay from his dark jeans. A black baseball cap shielded his face, but if she had to guess, he donned a serious scowl. He plucked several thorns from his dusty black T-shirt. *Ouch.*

His eyes never met hers when he said, "Damn, lady. All of that road and you nearly plow me down."

"I'm so sorry. I didn't see—"

When his brown-eyed gaze leveled on her, Gadiya's mouth went dry. Were her eyes playing tricks on her? Her brain certainly was. Maybe the combination of adrenaline and the mid-June heat confused her. Had she bumped her head on the steering wheel? Now she was just grasping for straws, grasping for anything that would explain this.

"Gadiya?"

No, this was definitely no mirage. Though she wished like hell it was.

Nico. The word wouldn't go any farther than her thoughts.

She should have instantly recognized Nico's muscled frame. It had been a couple of years, but a body like his—sturdy and commanding—you didn't forget. Thirty-one had been good to him. The temperature rose several degrees as her eyes roamed over every inch of his smooth, dark skin.

Relief, fear, yearning, and anger all coursed through her simultaneously, her body confused by the contrasting reactions. It wasn't sure if it was supposed to appreciate the well-put-together man in front of her or despise him.

The latter worked.

Needing to put distance between herself and Nico, Gadiya turned on her heels and stalked away, leaving her ex flat on his ass. The same way he'd left her two years ago.

***

Nico Dupree never imagined his first hour back in Mount Pleasance would involve a broken-down vehicle, a dead cell phone, and almost getting run down by his ex. Her mouth had said accident, but her snarl screamed attempted murder. And he could have sworn she'd revved the engine right before the muscle car had come barreling toward him.

Damn, she was still as fiery and gorgeous as he remembered. Even more beautiful, if that was possible. The impact of her presence stalled his brain. When it slowly rebooted, he shuffled to his feet, ignoring the pain in his leg and shooting through his shoulder.

Her swift departure answered a question he'd yet to ask. She still hated him. "Gadiya, wait."

She continued to make haste toward her vehicle. "Why? You don't need medical attention. And you obviously can walk."

"Can I at least get an apology?"

Gadiya kicked up a cloud of dust when she stopped. She turned and glared at him. In hindsight... But he'd gotten what he wanted, for Gadiya to stop. Her expression could easily be construed as lethal, like moments before a predator pounced on its prey. He hadn't needed medical attention a short while ago, but something told him he just might need it soon.

"An apology?" She released a menacing laugh. "*You* want an apology from *me*?"

Well, he couldn't let her see him sweat now. There

was no other choice but to follow through, despite the feeling of impending doom. "Yes. You did nearly turn me into a hood ornament."

Gadiya's jaw shifted from side to side. From experience, he knew that was a bad sign. But instead of lashing out at him—as he'd expected—she smiled, which elevated the situation from bad to worse. She was too damn calm. He slid a casual glance at their surroundings. She could kill him and bury him along this desolate stretch, and no one would discover his body until he was merely bone fragments. And who would miss him?

Calmly, she said, "You're right, Nico. I do owe you an apology. I am so sorry for almost hitting you."

Based on her icy expression, he questioned the sincerity of the statement. Now was being cordial to him so difficult? Of course, he didn't allow the words to roll past his lips. "Thank you."

"And I'm thankful," she added.

Nico arched a brow. "Thankful?" Did this mean she was happy to see him, after all? A wave of delight rippled through him.

"Yes, thankful. Because had I realized it was you, I would not have missed. I don't think prison would look good on me."

Gadiya turned and started away again, mumbling something under her breath.

He tried to keep his eyes above her waist, but he couldn't prevent them from roaming to her ass in those form-fitting khaki shorts she wore. Her long legs didn't skip a beat escaping him. On her heels, he said, "You don't mean that."

Snatching open the driver's side door, she said, "Trust me, I do." She slid behind the wheel and cranked the engine. The muscle car roared to life. The vehicle was just as sexy as she was.

"I'm having car trouble. Can I at least get a ride into town?" It was the least she could do.

"Enjoy your walk."

Walk? It was at least another ten miles before he reached civilization. With the way his leg was throbbing, he wouldn't get there before nightfall. And it wasn't like he could call for help, seeing how he'd forgotten to charge his phone, and it'd died over an hour ago.

Damn. Karma is truly a sneaky witch.

Wait, why was he stressing? Gadiya wouldn't leave him stranded on the side of the road in the middle of nowhere. When her hand rested on the gearshift, he frowned. Would she? A beat later, he had his answer in the form of a cloud of white smoke. He coughed and waved his hand in front of his nose. Then again, maybe she would.

Apparently, she still held one helluva grudge. But could he blame her? Clearly, time didn't heal all wounds. Hell, it hadn't even patched Gadiya's.

Once Gadiya's car disappeared around the bend, Nico hobbled to Hilda—his 1977 Chevrolet Silverado truck. He patted the side of the primed gray hunk of metal. "I'm not sure who's more temperamental, girl, you or Gadiya."

He tossed another glance in the direction Gadiya had traveled, holding out a minute amount of hope that she'd feel sympathy for him and return. Nothing but open road greeted him. Securing Hilda, he grabbed a bottle of water from the cooler in the back and started his long trek.

Nico understood Gadiya's disdain toward him. He'd be the first to admit he'd done her wrong. He'd been a damn fool to ever lose the love of that woman.

Pushing the past from his thoughts, he balked under the brutal rays of the midday sun that felt as if it was cooking him from the inside out. Removing his shirt, he stuffed it in the back of his waistband. Of all days to wear black. A trail of sweat trickled down his back and rolled between his shoulder blades.

If he died of heat stroke, he'd come back and haunt Gadiya for the rest of her life. Hell, right now, that seemed like the only way he'd get to spend any time with her.

When Nico rounded the bend, he stopped dead in his tracks. Gadiya's car sat idling on the side of the road. Was she there for him? Of course she was. What other reason could there be? Well, there was one. Maybe she intended to finish what she'd started. He wasn't entirely convinced she hadn't known it was him as she'd suggested.

"Could you hurry up? I don't have all day. Plus, it's hot out here."

Her shaded eyes stayed trained forward, never glancing in his direction as she spoke. He broke into a jog. It was painful as hell, but he couldn't risk her changing her mind and peeling off again. Inside, the scorching hot burgundy leather seat fried his back. *"Ow."*

A twitch played at the corner of Gadiya's mouth as if she was holding back a laugh. Clearly, she found pleasure in his pain.

"You're getting me wet." Her body tensed. "Getting it wet. My seat. You're getting sweat on my seat," she said in an exhausted whisper.

It seemed he wasn't the only one having lustful thoughts. "In that case, I guess I should put on my shirt." He pulled the black fabric over his head, wincing from the shoulder pain. "Don't want to get anything else wet."

Gadiya fisted the steering wheel and punched the gas. Nico was sure they'd go careening off the side of the road. But thankfully, she maintained control. *Whew.* He snatched the seatbelt and fastened it quickly.

As they traveled, Nico didn't hide his perusal of Gadiya. He'd seen her plenty of times in his dreams—and fantasies—over the years, but to actually see her in the flesh was a caress to his soul. And what tempting flesh it was.

She hadn't changed much at all. Still a body that could stop traffic. Still as gorgeous as a baby doll. Still able to create a hunger inside of him that made him weak in the knees. His eyes traveled along her almond-toned skin and wished it were his hands making the journey instead.

Her ample breasts strained against the white fabric of her tank top. His mouth watered at the idea of pulling one of her nipples between his lips. His gaze moved slowly down her frame, appreciating every supple inch of her. Heat swirled in the pit of his stomach. Time may have passed, but his attraction to Gadiya hadn't waned one bit. He got the feeling that he wasn't the only one feeling a vibe.

"What are you looking at?" Gadiya said, her tone as corrosive as acid.

When Nico's eyes rose to hers, she turned away. Why couldn't she look at him? Was she afraid he'd peer through those dark tinted glasses and see her desire? "Are you seeing anyone?"

On a scale from one to ten—ten being the worse—this question ranked one hundred in the most dim-witted questions ever asked category. But, hell, he wanted—even needed—to know the answer. The last he'd heard she was single, but that had been over a year ago.

The idea of another man pleasuring her angered him, which was totally ridiculous. Had he really expected her to wait on him to come to his damn senses and realize she'd been the best thing to ever happen to him? And that was no exaggeration.

Gadiya whipped her head toward him. "How is that any of your business?"

He shrugged. "I was just making small talk."

"Don't. Silence is perfectly okay with me. And anyway, wouldn't 'how have you been since I bolted on you without as much as a goodbye' have been more appropriate?"

Yeah, he deserved that. "How have you been, Gadiya?"

"Great, Nico. And yourself?"

From the mock dripping from her words, he doubted she gave a damn how he'd been. "We really need to talk."

"No, we don't. We have absolutely nothing to talk about."

Nico started to dispute the claim because, despite what Gadiya believed, they had plenty to discuss. But clearly, now was not a good time for her. But he would get his day, and he would get his woman.

2

Gadiya shot a scowl at her soon-to-be ex-older sister. This was Gadiya's kitchen. How was Rana going to stand in it and insult her in such a manner? And on a Sunday. A day of peace, nonetheless.

Peace? Really? Who was she kidding? Gadiya hadn't experienced a moment of peace since discovering Nico was back in town. He was a distraction she could definitely do without.

And why in the hell did he still have to look so damn good?

She wasn't sure what she'd done to the Universe to piss it off, but she was ready to apologize on bended knee if it meant she would never have to see Nico again.

"It's just the two of us here, Gadi. Go 'head and admit it."

Gadiya ignored the silly smirk on Rana's soft brown face. Slamming down the wooden spoon she'd been holding, she huffed. "For the last time, I am *not* still in love with Nico Dupree. He is a thing of my past."

"Really? Sooo, is that why we've spent the last hour talking about...the past?"

Gadiya shot a narrow-eyed gaze at Rana. "I really hate you right now." She jabbed a finger toward the door. "Get out."

Both women burst into laughter.

The threat was only idle. Gadiya loved her sister, both her sisters. Though she didn't get to see Sadona, the eldest Lassiter sister, a lot since she and her husband had made the move several hours away to Wilmington, North Carolina.

"You'd have to get the National Guard to remove me from this stool. Especially with the feast you've prepared." Rana reached over in an attempt to snag a deviled egg but snatched her hand back when Gadiya popped it. "Ouch."

"Wash your hands," Gadiya warned.

Rana pouted and moved to the sink. "So, did Nico say what he's doing back in Mount Pleasance? Though I have my suspicions why."

When Gadiya glanced over at her sister, Rana grinned. Gadiya ignored what she suspected Rana was implying—that Nico was possibly back for her. If by some ridiculous chance that was the case—though she found it highly unlikely—he was wasting his precious time.

"He didn't say. I didn't ask. It doesn't matter."

If Gadiya was being truly honest—at least with herself—she had to admit that she'd been minimally curious as to why Nico had returned. He no longer had family in Mount Pleasance. Maybe he intended to sell his parents' home. It had set empty since he'd been gone. Now *that* made sense, more sense than his return having anything to do with her.

Well, if he planned to get market value for the brick Victorian, he was definitely going to have to give it

15

some TLC. The place was gorgeous but needed work. She'd once imagine them growing old together there.

"Gadiya? Gadiya!"

When Rana snapped two fingers in Gadiya's face, she swatted them away. "What?"

"Are you daydreaming about the past?"

Rana laughed, but Gadiya didn't share in her amusement. "I'm this close to disowning you." She pinched together two fingers.

Rana claimed a deviled egg and leaned against the counter. "So, how does Nico look? Is he still the epitome of delicious sin."

Gadiya shrugged nonchalantly. "He looks all right." Who in the hell was she kidding? When she'd gotten a glimpse of Nico shirtless, her entire body hummed. It would have been so much easier to ignore him if he'd ballooned to seven hundred pounds. But no. He'd gone and kept himself in tip-top shape—bulging arms, sculpted chest, washboard abs. Rana's words drew her back to their conversation.

"Just all right?" Rana questioned.

Gadiya refused to look at her sister. "Okay. Maybe a little better than all right. And maybe I was a wee bit attracted to him. Any woman with a pulse would have been. But my reaction is a far cry from being in love with him."

"Can you honestly look me in the eyes and say you don't still feel something for Nico? You two were...perfect together."

Sadness filled Gadiya. "Obviously not. He walked

away, remember? When I needed him most, he abandoned me. I loved him so much, Rana. He destroyed me." Gadiya cleared her throat when her voice cracked. Regaining some semblance of strength, she said, "I'll never love Nico Dupree again."

Rana's tone was soft and comforting when she said, "Phoenix was his best friend, Gadiya. It—"

"I don't want to talk about this, Rana!" Gadiya closed her eyes and swallowed the emotions raging inside of her. The past was the past. Why was she the only one wanting to keep it there? Opening her eyes, she faced Rana. "Can we just enjoy lunch? Please?"

Rana wrapped her arms around Gadiya. "I'm sorry. I didn't mean to upset you. I just... I love you, and I want to see you happy."

How did Rana ever believe she could be happy with Nico? "I know. And I love you, too."

Nico had only been in town a day and was already causing a disruption in her life. Mount Pleasance wasn't humongous, but it was big enough that she'd hopefully be able to avoid her past—Nico—the only man she'd ever loved.

***

Nico's first stop after getting Hilda running was the Mount Pleasance Cemetery. This visit was long overdue. A myriad of emotions caused chaos inside of him as he stood at the foot of his best friend's gravesite. Even after two years, the pain still lingered. He still couldn't believe Phoenix was gone, nor did he want to believe it.

Nico eased onto the warm ground, propping his back against the granite headstone. "What's up, bro? Guess who's back in town. Yep, me. Sorry it's taken me two years to get here, but your death took me through some things."

Nico stared across the green at an older, gray-haired man placing flowers down. The man touched two trembling fingers to his lips, then rested them against the heart-shaped headstone. His wife, maybe? Nico's chest tightened. Nico understood the man's pain. Though Gadiya hadn't died, her love for him had. That was just as bad.

"Guess who was the first person I ran into—or should I say who nearly ran into me?" Nico chuckled. "Your sister." The recall caused a warm sensation to flow through him. "I didn't think that woman could get any more beautiful. I was wrong."

Nico snagged a dandelion and plucked at the yellow petals. It was odd, but being there—bearing his soul to a dead man—gave him a sense of peace he hadn't experienced in a long time.

"If you're looking down from heaven, I know you're probably pretty pissed at me. I swore I'd never hurt her. Unfortunately, that's exactly what I ended up doing. I broke the heart of the only woman who's ever truly believed in me."

Nico tapped his head back against the hard stone as if knocking some sense into himself. "I regret losing her, man. Every damn—" He chastised himself for swearing in a cemetery. As if he needed any more bad luck to reign down on him. "Every day of my life I live with the consequences of my actions."

A warm breeze kicked up, sending a cyclone of leaves swirling around him. It reminded him of how Gadiya's highlighted locks had blown in the wind as they drove to town in her convertible. He chuckled. "Believe it or not, P, I'm under some crazed delusion that I can get her to love me again. But recalling our initial encounter, I'm not so sure that's possible."

As if Phoenix was sitting right beside him, Nico could hear him saying: *Anything is possible. You just have to be willing to take the chance.*

Nico lowered his head. "I miss her, P. I miss everything about her. The gentle way she smoothed her hand down my cheek every morning and kissed the tip of my nose. The way she soothed me when I was stressed. Hearing her say, I love you. Watching her sleep. Kissing her. Falling asleep in her arms."

His jaws tightened as regret jolted through him. He'd screwed up majorly. If he could only turn back the hands of time, erase his selfish act. Of course, at the time, he hadn't seen it as him being selfish. He'd seen it as punishment he deserved.

"I still love Gadiya with everything inside of me that's good. But she hates me." He released a single laugh. "We both know how stubborn your sister can be. There's no way in hell— there's no way she'd ever forgive me." He'd seen that much in her eyes. Hell, he hadn't forgiven himself. And maybe she shouldn't either.

Tilting his head back, Nico stared toward heaven. "Phoenix, man...why?" he whispered. "Why did you do it?" Nico couldn't understand how in the hell a man who radiated so much light in everyone's life could be silently suffering from so much darkness in his own?

"I don't care what anyone says about suicide condemning the soul to eternal hellfire, I know you're strolling the golden roads of heaven, P. God would never allow the devil to have you." Nico's eyes clouded with tears. "But I wish he would send you back long enough for me to tell you face-to-face that I'm so sorry for not being there for you. I should—"

Nico lunged from his seated position, swatting at his head. When he turned to see what had swooped past him, a cardinal was perched on top of Phoenix's headstone.

"Shoo, bird." When the creature didn't budge a red feather, Nico fanned his hand toward it. "Go on, nice birdie. Fly away."

Still, North Carolina's state bird refused to move. Deciding the headstone wasn't big enough for the two of them, Nico said his goodbyes to Phoenix and promised to return soon. On the walk back to Hilda, one face played in his thoughts. Gadiya's.

Anything is possible. You just have to be willing to take the chance.

He'd never shied away from a challenge. No need in starting now.

3

Gadiya found a park, exited, and made her way across the freshly paved parking lot of the Mount Pleasance Fire Department. If they had money in the budget for asphalt, they surely had money in the budget to afford her services. She was cutting them one helluva deal. And it was exactly what she intended to tell them, in a gentler manner, of course.

She'd allotted another week for someone to get back to her—which no one had. She refused to wait around another day. Yes, she understood the new fire chief had only been there a week and probably had far more pressing issues to handle, but all she needed was ten minutes of his time to convince him she was the right choice to present to the council.

Waiting was yielding her no results. One thing she'd declared a long time ago was she'd never trust another man to have her back. That only led to disappointment.

An image of Nico played in her head, and she chastised her body for the slight tingle in her belly. She'd done a good job avoiding him over the past week. With any luck, she'd continue the streak.

Instead of using the main entrance, Gadiya entered through the fire engines' bay. Ollie—her supposed contact—stood chatting with Brill, another MPFD fireman. One thing she could say about whoever did the hiring for the MPFD, they sure knew how to pick 'em. Tall, chocolate, fit, and heavenly on the eyes. They'd make one hell of a monthly calendar spread.

Ollie paused mid-laugh when he spotted her approaching. *You get more flies with honey than vinegar*, she reminded herself, then replaced her tight expression with a hundred watt smile.

"Ollie? Nice to see you."

"Gadiya? What are you doing here?"

Despite his chiseled looks, he wasn't the brightest. What in the hell did he think she was doing there? Adhering to her mild-mannered approach, she said, "I was in the neighborhood. Thought I'd swing by and chat with your new boss." She pointed over her shoulder. "Is he in?"

Ollie eyed her like a deer in the headlights. "Ahh..."

"Yes, he is."

Gadiya froze, the familiar voice raking over her skin like a subtle warm breeze. She turned to see Nico standing several feet away, his arms crossed over his chest. A neutral expression played on his face as if he'd somehow expected her. His eyes raked quickly over her yellow The Twisted Balloon T-shirt and khaki shorts.

Gadiya's eyes devoured him. He looked even better with a hat not shadowing his features. The tucked in red tee he wore fitted his toned body with precision. The fabric stretched to accommodate the mounds at his biceps. The black cargo-style pants revealed little about what lie beneath, but she already knew—muscular legs, powerful thighs, and a long, thick—

A radio crackled somewhere nearby snapping her back to her senses. Stiffening her back, she regained focus. What was Nico doing there? Then it dawned on her. Maybe he was volunteering again. Ignoring his devastatingly good looks, she said, "I'm here to see the fire chief."

Nico neared her and her skin prickled. *Get it together, girl. Don't reveal that he has any effect on you.*

"I heard." He cocked a brow. "Do we have an appointment?"

"Do we—? Wait, *you're* the new fire chief?"

He nodded. "Yes. Is that a problem?"

She wanted to scream, *you're damn right it's a problem*, but instead, said, "Why would that be a problem?"

He shrugged. "Given our previous encounter…"

His words trailed off, eyes gliding past her. When she followed his stare, Ollie and Brill turned away. She scowled at their backs. What had they been doing behind her?

"Let's talk in my office."

Giving a single nod, she followed Nico inside. A lounge area with a brown leather couch, several straight-back chairs, and a wall-mounted television was arranged on one side of the spacious room, while a kitchen with a lengthy dining table was positioned on the opposite. For some reason, she expected a Dalmatian dog to come galloping toward them.

"Gadiya Lassiter?"

Gadiya instantly recognized that smooth baritone voice. She turned, a smile curling her lips. "Colton Chesapeake?"

Colton was fire chief in neighboring Indigo Falls. They'd dated all of a month, discovering they made better friends than lovers. She was sure she'd made plenty women happy when she unleashed him back into the world.

Colton was still as handsome as a male model. Flawless milk chocolate skin, entrancing brown eyes, and an infectious smile. The true sign of a Chesapeake man. With a fluid movement, he wrapped her in a tight embrace.

When they pulled apart, she said, "What are you doing in Mount Pleasance?"

Colton eyed Nico, whose gaze was pinned to Gadiya. "Getting the new fire chief up to speed."

Nico's scrutiny unnerved Gadiya, but she didn't know why. Ignoring the perplexed expression on his face, she turned back to Colton. "You two know each other?"

"Yeah, we met about a year ago at a conference in DC," Colton said.

"DC." Is that where Nico had escaped to? Nico never uttered a word, simply continued to level her with his hard stare. Gadiya nodded. "Ah."

"Well, I gotta get out of here. Nico, man, if you need me, you know how to reach me," Colton said.

Colton's words finally pulled Nico's attention away

from Gadiya, and she breathed a silent sigh of relief. Why in the hell did she give one damn about the conclusion she was sure Nico had jumped to about her and Colton. If anything, she should have found pleasure in his assumption.

Nico offered Colton his hand. "Thanks for swinging by, man. I appreciate it."

"Like I said, anytime you need me." Colton slid his attention back to Gadiya. "It's been a while. I'd love to catch up."

"I've got your number. I'll definitely give you a ring," she said.

Two minutes later, Gadiya stood in Nico's office—a room scattered with boxes, piles of papers, and files. The place was a fire hazard. Strike a match and the entire room would go up in a blaze of glory.

"Excuse the mess," Nico said. "I've been sifting through all of this stuff. I believe the guy before me was a paper packrat."

And an asshole, she thought. *You should fit right in*.

Nico's words were cordial but dry. Had her interaction with Colton pissed him off? If so, why? It wasn't like she knew they were friends when she'd briefly dated Colton. Wait, why was she justifying her actions? Nico left her, not the other way around. She was free to date anyone she chose. However, she would have never knowingly dated one of his friends.

Why was she feeling so guilt-ridden?

It was a sign. An indication that being here with

Nico was a bad idea. She could feel it in her spirit. Did she really need this contract? It only took her a second to answer. Yes. Yes, she did. With all of the news coverage the event would garner, it would give her infant company just the publicity boost it needed. At least, that's what she was hoping.

I can do this. It's nothing but business as usual.

Nico directed her to one of the chairs at the small, round conference table. Once seated, he occupied the chair right next to her. Why in the hell did he have to sit so close?

"Thank you for taking—"

"So, you and Colton Chesapeake?"

Gadiya's first instinct had been to debunk his insinuation but decided against it. She didn't owe Nico Dupree any explanations. "I'm here to discuss my proposal. I don't readily see how my love life fits into the conversation, do you?"

It was subtle, but she saw the tightening of his jaw. The idea of her and Colton angered him. Or maybe it was her reluctance to discuss it. Or both.

"You're right. As always," he said.

Something about the *as always* comment felt like a jab, but she ignored it.

Nico crossed an ankle over his knee and rested one arm on the table. "So, what do you need from me, Ms. Lassiter?"

Ms. Lassiter. Cute. "I don't need *anything* from you, *Mr. Dupree*. However, I would like the opportunity to provide the kids' entertainment for the upcoming

Fireman's Day Celebration. There would be—"

"Ah. So you *do* need something from me. You need me to get this approved by the council. Am I correct?"

In that instance, something—perhaps the smirk on his face, coupled with the look of triumph—told her Nico was not going to make this easy for her. But if he wanted a fight, she'd give him one.

***

Nico did his best to remain professional, but with Gadiya sitting so close to him, professional was the last thing on his mind. If the strained expression on her face was any indication, she was imagining several ways to kill him.

Obviously, she didn't like the idea of needing him. That made two of them not liking the idea of something. He didn't like the notion of her having slept with Colton Chesapeake or any other man. The thought was like razor-sharp nails clawing down his spine. He had no right in the world to feel scorned, but he did. That foolish male pride—or ego. Either fit.

Nico sighed, softening his approach. "Look, Gadiya, I know you don't like the idea of—"

"With all due respect, Mr. Dupree, you haven't been around for a while. I don't think you know what I like."

"I may not have been around, but don't get it twisted, *Ms. Lassiter*. There's not another man on this planet who knows you or your body better than I do," Nico shot back.

Gadiya eyed him as if she couldn't believe he'd gone there. And frankly, neither could he.

A patronizing expression spread across her confident face. "Yeah, well that was a long time ago. My tastes have definitely matured since then."

By matured tastes, he assumed she'd been referring to Colton Chesapeake, because she tossed a mischievous glance toward the door, then hummed a sound of pleasure. A fireball of fury ignited inside him as jealousy threatened to turn him to ashes.

He chuckled, rubbing his index and middle fingers across his bottom lip. Everything inside of him warned to pull back from her inflaming words, but the skilled fireman side of his brain wouldn't allow him to. "You think two years has made it less likely that I'm still your flavor? Less likely that I still know every damn inch of your beautiful body?"

The confidence Gadiya displayed moments before seemed to lose much of its potency. Her hard expression morphed into something more delicate. He should have stopped chipping away at her armor, but he didn't.

"I may not have had the pleasure of physically being with you, Gadiya, but I've touched you every single day in my thoughts. I've tasted you in my fantasies. Made love to you in my dreams. Two years hasn't made me less familiar with your body; it's made me more."

Gadiya stared at him speechless for a moment or two, then jumped to her feet. "I-I have to go."

Nico came to his feet, hooking Gadiya around the waist. Apparently, she couldn't take the heat, but he wasn't ready for her to escape the kitchen. Pulling her body flush to him, he held her there. His body protested having her so close, but he couldn't let her go. Plus, she didn't seem overly eager to be freed.

He wanted her, every inch. And he would take her right there in his office if she allowed him. "I may not be too appetizing to you now, Gadiya, but you still have a taste for me. I can see it in your eyes."

"Then you should seriously consider getting glasses."

Her tone held less bite than before. Nico almost thought he'd heard a hint of surrender in her tone, but he didn't wager on it. Gadiya would never make things this easy for him. But despite how hard she tried to fight it, he knew he had just as much of an effect on her body as she had on his.

Resting his hands on her waist, he turned her to face him. The impact of her mouth so close to his was like an iron fist to the chest. Many nights he'd imagine being this close to her again. Now, here they stood. "I know your body, Gadiya. I know if I kiss you on the space below your earlobe, your nipples will harden like jewels."

Gadiya arched a defiant brow. "If you try to kiss me *anywhere*, it's not *my* jewels you'll need to worry about."

He chuckled. Still as spunky as ever. With the tip of his finger, he drew a delicate line along the side of her face, ignoring her threat. "And if I kissed along your jaw line, then dragged my tongue down the column of your neck, I guarantee you'd get wet for me."

Gadiya's breathing grew ragged, and he smiled to himself. Though this hadn't been his intent when he'd invited her to his office, he was enjoying watching her get turned on.

"I most certainly would not," she said.

"You're in denial."

"And you're wasting your time. Your what-if scenarios will *never* happen. Now if you will kindly get out of my way..."

Nico allowed Gadiya to escape his hold. He may not have broken her shell, but he'd surely cracked it. As she made her way across the floor, he said, "I'll tell you what's a waste of time. Your fighting this. You have a right to be pissed at me, Gadiya, but you can't deny you still feel something for me."

This stopped her in her tracks. Whipping around, she charged him like a raging bull. "Anything I may have felt for you in the past is long gone. I feel nothing for you now, Nico Dupree. *Nothing*. And I never will."

"Is that why you're still single?" He regretted the words the moment they escaped. There could have been a myriad of reasons why she wasn't in a relationship, none of them having anything to do with him.

Gadiya slowly shook her head, something in her

expression turning sad. "The reason I'm still single has nothing to do with you. But if you must know, I decided to never give my heart to another man, because the one man I trusted with it, shattered it into tiny pieces. I loved that jerk, that coward, far more than he deserved. I loved him far more than breathing, which was okay, because, with him, I never feared suffocating. He gave me life. Then he took it away."

Nico hadn't expected her powerful summation. He couldn't speak, couldn't move toward her, could hardly breathe. All he could do was dumbly stare into her glistening eyes, then at her back as she turned to leave.

Gadiya stopped at the door. Over her shoulder, she said, "On second thought, I guess my being single has everything to do with you. I never want to see you again, Nico. You are dead to me. Just like the idea of me ever loving you again."

With that, she was gone.

When the door clicked shut, Nico leaned against his desk, slain by Gadiya's words. Was he mounting a war for her love that couldn't be won?

4

It had been two days, and Gadiya still hadn't gotten over her blowup with Nico at the firehouse. She slapped an open palm against her desk. How could she have allowed him to get under her skin like that? She should have ignored his baiting words and just kept walking. Why did she have to entertain his foolishness?

With only a sentence he'd forced her to relive their past, expose her hurt, admit the adverse effect his betrayal had had on her. She closed her eyes and massaged at the faint throb in her temple.

Stupid. Stupid. Stupid.

She wasn't sure what had come over her. Feelings she'd thought were long gone rushed back and… She shook her head. The horrible things she'd said to him.

How could so many emotions swirl inside of her at once—fear, hurt, anger. Some of that anger returned when she recalled his words. Where in the hell did he get off suggesting she still felt something for him? Though it may be true, he—of all people—had no right to say it.

I know you and your body. Maybe at one point he did. She'd give him that much. At one point, he'd been able to command her body with a brown-eyed gaze. But that was then. This was now. Now…she was the one in control. Or so she desperately wanted to believe.

Bastard.

Gadiya reclined, rested her head against the back of the chair, and closed her eyes. An image of the enemy filled her thoughts. In his office, Nico had been so damn close to her she could hardly breathe. No wonder her brain had gone on hiatus. It had been oxygen deprived. She hated how good it felt when he'd hooked her around the waist and drew her close to him. The surge of energy she'd experienced had nearly buckled her knees.

So, you do need me.

Her eyes popped open. "Dammit." She didn't want to think about him or how good she'd felt in his arms. She didn't want to consider the fact that—despite what she'd said—she did need him. In all honesty, she didn't want to even acknowledge he existed in her world. But how in the hell could she deny it when lately, he was all she thought about?

What sorcery was he working on her?

Black, sexy magic, an inner voice taunted.

Ugh.

One of Gadiya's interns called over the speaker phone. "Gadiya?"

"Yes, Ciara?"

"There's a Nico Dupree on the line for you."

Gadiya's brain stalled. What could he possibly want? Probably to continue where they'd left off. She didn't have the time or temperament to go another round with him. "I'm sorry to ask you to lie for me, but could you please tell him I'm in a meeting?"

"Sure thing."

Gadiya massaged her now pounding temple. What did she do about her Nico problem? She wouldn't be able to avoid him forever. And if the city council approved her proposal, she'd be forced to interact with him.

"Gadiya?" Ciara's voice danced over her speaker again.

What now? "Yes."

"Mr. Dupree says to let you know he'll be meeting with the council soon and will have an answer for you by the end of the week."

How noble of him. "That sounds good."

"Oh…"

Gadiya sighed heavily to herself. *Now what?*

"He also said to have an ugly day."

Gadiya tried to bite back her smile, but it broke through despite her efforts. "Thanks, Ciara."

Every morning, Nico would tell her to have a beautiful day, unless they'd had a silly argument the night before. Then he'd tell her to have an ugly day, which actually translated to have a beautiful one, which he couldn't say because he had to keep up with the hard façade.

Yeah, it was silly, but it had been their thing.

"Damn you for coming back into my life, Nico."

Things were so much simpler when he was out of sight. She'd had no problem keeping him out of mind. Now, she couldn't keep him off her mind.

***

Nico's last order of business with the city council was the proposal Gadiya had submitted for the Fireman's Day celebration. According to Ollie, she'd been waiting close to two months for an answer. Getting her proposal approved had to earn him some brownie points. When it came to Gadiya, he could use all the advantages he could get.

Clearly, she was still pissed at him. When he'd reached out to her a couple of days ago, she'd refused to take his call. She'd had her employee give him some lame excuse about being in a meeting. *Meeting? Yeah, right.* She was avoiding him.

Redirecting his attention, he scanned the seven council members—three woman and four men—as they mulled over the copy of the proposal he'd provided to each of them.

Chairwoman Stephens was the first to speak up, "We'd love to approve this, Chief, but it's over the budget we've allotted for the kids' portion of the entertainment."

"It's a little over, but—"

"A little? Son, it's close to two thousand dollars over. Ain't nothing *little* about that," Mr. Hicks chimed in. "We've received several more reasonable proposals that I feel—"

"Yes, but The Twisted Balloon is local." *Damn.* He didn't mean to sound so combative. He wasn't there to make enemies. Especially with the people who held the power to fire him.

"Chief Dupree is right," said Chairwomen Stephens. "The Twisted Balloon is local, which is a plus. We wholeheartedly support our local small businesses, when we can. But our hands are tied here, Chief. Unless, of course, we can get this proposal under the allotted budget."

According to one of the line items, Gadiya had already applied a thirty percent discount. How much more could she discount without taking a loss? No one was in business to lose money. This wasn't how he'd expected this to go. Without giving it much consideration, Nico said, "I'll cover the amount over the budget."

Chairwoman Stephens arched a brow but didn't question his offer. The same couldn't be said about Mr. Hicks, who jumped right in. If Nico hadn't known any better, he'd think the man had something against him.

"That's mighty generous of you, son. But we can't allow that. There are—"

"Herbert, if the Chief wants to contribute to the enjoyment of the Mount Pleasance youth, who are we to deny it? I don't see a thing wrong with it." Giving Mr. Hicks the side-eye, she said, "If more of the great citizens of Mount Pleasance were as charitable, we'd have a more adequate budget."

This clammed Mr. Hicks right up. Obviously, he was one of those less charitable citizens she referred to.

Chairwoman Stephens continued, "All those in favor say aye."

A chorus of ayes sounded from the other

members. Mr. Hicks aged brown skin crinkled into a frown, but he went along with the others, spitting out a barely audible aye.

"The ayes have it." Chairwoman Stephens banged her gavel down. "Meeting adjourned."

Nico thanked the council and made his way out of the courthouse. Only he could come out of a meeting owing money. But it was for a good cause. Making his way across the square, he appreciated the mild eighty-two degrees. It was in stark comparison to the scorcher that had greeted him when he'd first arrived in town.

"Chief. Oh, Chief Dupree."

Nico turned and squinted against the sun. A short, portly woman came into view, moving with purpose toward him. Her flowered dress brushed the ground as she walked, and her jet-black hair bounced with each step she took.

"Hello, Chief. I'm Mary Augustine. I was just on my way to the firehouse to see you. You've saved me the trip. These old bones certainly appreciate you for it." She released a hearty laugh that seemed odd coming from her, given her delicate voice.

"Ah, nice to meet you, Ms. Augustine."

"It's *Mrs.*, but you wouldn't have known that."

"My apologies, ma'am."

"No harm done. The old chief and I were good friends. I hope we can be, as well."

He'd heard the old fire chief had been a rolling stone. Nico didn't know if Mrs. Augustine had been one of his conquests, so he wasn't sure how to respond to her comment. He simply smiled.

"This is for you."

He graciously accepted the small food container. "Thank you."

"A little something from my kitchen. Banana pudding I whipped up just this morning. Even wrapped you up a spoon. You can walk and eat at the same time."

"Mmm. I love banana pudding."

"Nothing fancy. Just an old family recipe. Folk love my banana pudding. Say it's to die for. Make it every year for the annual church picnic. Are you a God-fearing man, Chief Dupree?"

"Y—"

"I bet you are. Are you married?"

"N—"

"It's a pity if you're not. You're as handsome as one of those magazine models."

Since he doubted he'd get a full sentence out, Nico didn't bother to response. He simply flashed another warm smile.

"You're sure not much for words, are you?" She squeezed his bicep. "The strong, silent type, I see."

Help.

"That's okay. Sometimes it's best to listen more and talk less. Well, I won't hold you, Chief. Got to get home to the babies. My boys get cranky when I don't have their meal prepared on time."

Mrs. Augustine seemed a bit...mature to still have boys she needed to cook for. Hey, it was none of his business.

They said their goodbyes.

Nico polished off the banana pudding before he'd made it back to the firehouse. It had been tasty, but it wasn't better than Gadiya's. She had always been able to throw down in the kitchen. When they were together, he'd had to double his workouts because she was constantly feeding him. Man, what he wouldn't give for one of her home-cooked meals right now. Microwave dinners were getting real old, real quick.

When Nico walked inside, he got several strange looks. His brows furrowed. "What?"

Ollie smirked. "You have a visitor in your office."

A visitor?

Nico made his way down the hall and into his office. He was stunned to see Gadiya pacing back and forth. She stopped when their eyes locked. A cooling sensation crept along his spine. Her presence was like a burst of energy.

Was she there to plunge the sword even deeper into his heart? "Gadiya?"

Silently, she lifted a long food storage container off the conference table and offered it to him.

"What's this?"

"A peace offering."

Nico popped the top off and smiled. The delicious aromas of chocolate and vanilla invaded his nostrils. What was it with women giving him food today? Not that he was complaining, but between the banana pudding Mrs. Augustine had given him and these cookies he planned to devour as soon as he could, he'd have to head back to their workout room before he left for the day. "Chocolate chip cookies."

She shrugged one shoulder. "They used to be your favorite."

"They still are. Especially yours."

Gadiya's gaze left him briefly. He assumed that somehow the comment had made her uncomfortable. That hadn't been his intent. It had actually been meant as a compliment. "You don't have to bribe me. Your proposal was approved today."

A smile lit her face. "Really?"

He nodded.

"That's great. I was concerned that even with the discount it would be over budget."

Nico rubbed his finger across his bottom lip. "Ah, no. They were fine with it."

Gadiya studied him a moment, then said, "I said some really awful things to you the other day. Hurtful things. Things I regret."

Yeah, she had cut deep. But he'd deserved it.

She fidgeted with her fingers. "Anyway. I just wanted to say I'm sorry."

"Thank you. Does this mean I'm back from the dead?"

A lazy smile twitched at her lips. "Enjoy the cookies."

"I'm sure I will."

When she turned to leave, he desperately wanted to say something, anything to get her to stay. But this was neither the time nor place for them to engage in another heated battle of wills. Moving after her, he said, "I'll walk you out."

They moved through the hall in silence. Nico's eyes stayed pinned to Gadiya as she exited the building, strolled across the lot, and slid behind the wheel of the Mustang.

"You're not really going to eat those cookies, are you?" came from behind Nico.

Nico glanced down at the container he was still holding, then eyed Brill over his shoulder. "Why wouldn't I? No one bakes cookies like Gadiya."

Brill flashed a pained expression. "I wouldn't do that if I were you, man."

"Why?"

"A woman who you say despises you all of a sudden brings you a batch of *homemade* cookies. You have seen that movie where the maid brings the evil white lady the chocolate pie with a little something extra baked inside, right? The term rat poison comes to mind."

Nico glanced down at the container. Brill had a point. But was Gadiya's hate for him so strong she'd try to poison him? Nah. Maliciousness was not in Gadiya's nature.

"Don't listen to this fool," Ollie said. "And if you're not going to eat them, I will."

When Ollie attempted to take the cookies from him, Nico held them out of reach. "No one eats Gadiya's cookies but me."

Ollie and Brill burst into laughter.

"Get y'all minds out of the gutter and get back to work," Nico playfully ordered.

Heading back to his office, he had to admit he worked with a good group of guys. They had fun when it was time for fun and worked when it was time to work. And worked hard. It was a far cry from his last job. There, no one did anything unless it benefitted them in some way.

Nico eased down into his desk chair and popped one of Gadiya's cookies into his mouth. "Mmm." She hadn't lost her touch. After enjoying several more cookies, he saved the rest for later and dove into the pile of papers mounded on his desk.

An hour later, Nico was still sorting through documents that should have been shredded eons ago. His eyes needed a rest. When he stood to stretch, a ping of pain shot through his intestines. A beat later, he darted from behind his desk and into the tin can of a bathroom in his office.

Several hours passed and Nico had spent the majority of them in and out of the bathroom. He'd endured the laughs and cracks of the other men in the firehouse about the tainted cookies before finally deciding to go home for the day.

He'd barely made it through the front door before another wave of discomfort knotted his stomach, forcing him to rush into the bathroom again.

Gadiya!

She'd played dirty. With what little energy he had

remaining, he made his way into his bedroom and dropped face first on the mattress. He fished his cell phone from his pocket and pressed in the number to The Twisted Balloon.

After several rings, Gadiya's unmistakable soft tone danced over the line. For a second, the sweet sound of her voice made him forget how livid he was at her. Her siren effect didn't last long. "What in the hell did you put in those cookies?"

"Hold, please."

"Don't put me— hello? Hello?"

Dammit, she put me on hold.

Super loud, super annoying circus-type music blared in his ear, causing his temple to pound even harder. After a minute or so, the stupid melody was stuck in his head. Finally, Gadiya returned to the line.

"Nico?"

There was no longer any background noise, so he assumed she'd gone to a more private location. "Did you bake me laxative cookies?"

"Laxative cookies?" Gadiya laughed, and laughed, and laughed.

"It's not funny, Gadiya. I've been in and out of the bathroom all day after eating your damn tainted cookies. It feels like a tiger is clawing its way out of my gut."

"My cookies weren't tainted. I've eaten them, and so have my employees. No one is suffering from IBS-D but you." Another round of laughter sounded over the phone.

Irritable Bowel Syndrome. He assumed the d stood for diarrhea. Oh, she thought she was real funny. "I'm glad you're finding amusement in agony."

Sobering, Gadiya said, "I didn't do anything to the cookies, Nico. You're not important enough for me to compromise my character."

Ouch. "Then why is my colon on fire."

In a subdued tone, she said, "Why are you asking me? I'm not a doctor. What else have you eaten today?"

"I had oatmeal for breakfast, a handful of chips, some banana pudding from a nice lady named Mrs. Augustine, *your* cookies..."

"*Whoa, whoa, whoa.* Did you say, Mrs. Augustine?"

"Yeah. Why?"

Gadiya barked a laugh. "No one eats Mrs. Augustine's cooking. She baked her husband a meatloaf, and he died two hours later."

Nico's head arched off the bed, a wave of concern jolting through him. "He died? From her cooking?" *Shit.* Maybe he should go to the hospital. He didn't want to end up like Mr. Augustine.

"Well, not exactly. She'd put so much salt in the meatloaf it raised his blood pressure, and he had a stroke. But still..."

Nico blew a sigh of relief. He thought Mrs. Augustine had mistaken rat poison for bread crumbs.

"Plus, she has like fifteen cats that *all* live in the house with her."

Were those the boys she'd been referring to earlier, who got cranky when they didn't have their meal on time? A visual of the cats walking all over the countertops and licking the utensil made his stomach churn. "Oh God. I have to go, Gadiya. Pray for me."

Nico dropped the phone and sprinted back to the place he'd spent the majority of his day. As ridiculous as it sounded, his discomfort was a small price to pay to hear Gadiya laugh again. The sound nourished his soul.

And the fact she'd stayed on the line with him for so long had been a good sign, right? He'd sworn he heard a hint of concern in her voice, too—beneath all of the laughter. He didn't care what Gadiya said. Deep down, she still felt something for him. And he intended to bring whatever it was to the surface. That's if he lived beyond tonight.

5

Gadiya stood on Nico's porch staring at the once vibrant red door. Her gaze traveled to the red, white, and blue plastic pharmacy bag she held. On her way home, she'd swung by and purchased a bottle of anti-diarrheal, a two-liter ginger ale, and crackers.

Uncertainty about ringing the bell flooded her. Why did she care if Nico was suffering? He was no longer her concern, hadn't been for years. Plus, in her opinion, explosive diarrhea served him right.

What in the hell am I doing here?

Well, she was already here. Might as well leave the items. Two seconds and she was out of there. Five seconds tops. She could handle Nico for that long. Stabbing at the doorbell, she waited for him to answer. After about fifteen seconds with no answer, she pressed the button again. Still nothing.

Huh.

Gadiya's gaze slid toward the driveway, and she saw the red Ford F250 truck with Mount Pleasance Fire Department Fire Chief scrolled on the side. His personal vehicle was there, as well, which meant if he'd gone some place, it had been on foot.

He could have gone out for the evening with friends. Or on a date. She ignored the twinge of jealousy the date idea elicited. With the way he sounded earlier, both scenarios were unlikely. No, she seriously doubted he'd left the house.

That brought her to another possibility. He was avoiding her. Again, that didn't seem feasible. They were on fairly decent terms. Well, decent-ish. He had accused her of poisoning him.

Nico being asleep made the most sense; in which case, she didn't want to wake him. Gadiya gnawed at the corner of her lip. Or… A vision of Nico sprawled across the bathroom floor—unconscious—played in her head.

Though she would have preferred to deny it, concern flooded her. Placing the bag down, she rummaged through her purse for her cell phone. But before she could locate it, the door crept open like a scene from a horror movie.

Nico peered out, a look of surprise playing across his fragile features. Her heart sank staring into his glossy, weak eyes. Whatever bug he was fighting was whooping his ass.

He squinted against the fading sunlight. "Gadiya? Hey."

His voice was croaky and weak. The longer she stared at him, the more empathetic she grew. *Give him the bag and go.* "Um…hey. Did I wake you?"

"No."

She flashed a skeptical expression.

Nico managed a puny chuckle. "Yeah, but it's okay." His movement was cautious when he took a step back and propped himself against the door. "Come in."

She didn't move. "I just stopped by to give you

this." She lifted the bag from the porch and offered it to him.

"What is it? Please don't say more cookies." He flashed a strained smile.

Gadiya chuckled. "*No*. Medicine for your stomach, ginger ale, crackers."

Appreciation spread across his face. "Thank you. I think the worst is over. But this will definitely help."

"That's good." Standing there had to be draining, so she decided to let him get back to bed. "Well, I should go. You need your rest."

"Wait."

Nico took a step toward her and wobbled. Instinctively, her arms shot out as if to catch him. "Whoa. Nico...are you okay?"

He closed his eyes and massaged his forehead. "Yeah. Just a little lightheaded. I'm fine."

"You're not fine, Nico. You can barely stand. We need to get you to the hospital. You're probably dehydrated and—"

"You know I hate going to the doctor, Gadiya. I just need to make it back to the bed and lie down. I'll be fine."

Men. Stubborn as hell. This one especially. "Suit yourself. But if you wake up dead, I'm going to say I told you so." She paused. "Okay, that made no sense at all, but you know what I'm trying to say."

"Not really, no." His dry lips twitched into a half-smile.

Gadiya sighed heavily to herself. *So much for five*

seconds. Stepping inside, she said, "Come on. Let's get you back to bed and get some liquids in you."

Nico didn't protest when she wrapped her arm around his waist and urged him to lean against her. When he draped his arm around her shoulders, she doused the warmth that flowed through her. The scent of cologne teased her senses, while his touch brought back illicit memories that sent a surge of seductive energy between her legs.

Snap out of it.

Their trip down the hall was a slow one. She was glad he was using one of the lower-level bedrooms, because, at this rate, it would have been next week before they made it up the winding staircase.

The leisurely stroll gave her time to assess the home she hadn't entered in years. Though the outside needed some work, the inside of The Dupree House was in pretty good condition. The hardwood floors could use a good buffing, and the place could use a good airing out and dusting. Other than that, it was livable. There were a lot of memories trapped inside those walls. Memories vying for space in her head right now, but she refused them occupancy.

Once they'd made it inside his bedroom, Nico dropped onto the mattress. "Damn. It feels like I've climbed a mountain. Thank you, Gadiya. I owe you."

When their gazes connected, she could see the sincerity in his eyes. "No, you don't."

They held each other's attention for a long, intense moment. Why couldn't she shake these feelings for him? How could he still make her feel all the sensations that only a lover should be able to elicit?

Finding a breath, she said, "I'll be right back," and exited the room before she suffocated on desire.

The large kitchen outfitted with stainless steel appliances was just as she remembered. Removing a glass from the cherry cabinet, she filled it with ice, then ginger ale. Instead of immediately returning to Nico, she rested her palms against the stone island and closed her eyes to gather her thoughts.

Don't get your feelings involved. It'll only lead to more heartache.

Gadiya tossed her head back and released a drawn out breath. When Nico had refused to go to the hospital, she should have simply said okay and left. But no, she had to play nurturer like they were still an item. She tried telling herself that helping her fellow man was the moral thing to do, but she wasn't sure it had anything to do with being honorable at all.

Snagging the anti-diarrheal medicine and a pack of crackers, she headed out of the kitchen and back to the bedroom. "Okay. Ice cold ginger ale, crackers, and tasty medicine. A meal fit for a king. Or a man suffering from IBS-D."

Nico's mouth lifted into a crooked smile. "You're really enjoying this, aren't you?"

"Are you suggesting that I'm finding pleasure in your discomfort?"

"Yes."

She smirked. "Maybe a little."

"That's cold."

"I'm kidding, I'm kidding."

Gadiya placed the items on the nightstand, then eased down onto the edge of the bed. Breaking the seal of the plastic bottle, she poured a dose of the chalky white liquid into the premeasured cup and passed it to him. "Bottoms up."

Nico reluctantly accepted the tiny cup. Closing his eyes, he downed it in one big gulp, then winced.

"Yum. Good boy." She held the glass to Nico's lips. "Now drink."

When Nico rested his hand atop hers to help guide the glass to his mouth, his touch caused her skin to tingle. She resisted pulling away. He downed only a few sips of the ginger ale, then fell back against the pillow. She started to urge him to drink more, but when he draped his arm over his forehead and closed his eyes, she let him be.

Gadiya placed the glass on the nightstand. "Do you think you can stomach a cracker or two?"

Nico shook his head.

She didn't press. Impulsively, her eyes roamed over Nico. His clean shaven face, his strong, square jaw, his kissable lips, his wide shoulders, his flat mid-section, even his crotch. The impression his manhood made against the black gym shorts he wore corrupted her thoughts. "I should go. Let you get some rest."

Nico's eyes snapped open. "Stay. Please. Just a little while longer. I could use the company. We can watch a movie."

Gadiya eyed Nico as if he'd spoken in a language she couldn't readily decipher. She would have laughed had she not believed he was serious. A movie? Really? Did he believe the suggestion of a movie would entice her to stay? This wasn't a date. Despite having this pity thing working for him, what made him think—in a million years—she'd ever crawl into bed with him?

"I understand if it's too difficult," he said.

Too difficult? What in the hell was that supposed to mean? Did he believe she couldn't handle being next to him? Like he was this irresistible entity that no woman could resist. Obviously, he hadn't glanced in the mirror. He wasn't exactly at his most appealing.

Then it hit her. He was attempting to bait her. Could he really believe she was that gullible? Did he really think his challenge words would prompt her to kick common sense aside and climb into bed with him? She hoped not.

However, she did have something to prove, but only to herself. She'd be damned if Nico got the upper hand. She needed to show him that she truly was over him, especially after that dismal display in his office.

Gadiya stepped out of her sandals, never breaking eye contact with Nico as she climbed in and anchored her back against the headboard. Playing it as cool as possible, she said, "So, what are we watching?"

"You choose. Remote's on the nightstand."

Gadiya flicked through the stations, stopping on a documentary about black bears.

"Really, Gadi? You know this is going to put me to

sleep, right?"

Precisely what she was banking on. She, too, could be crafty. Ignoring the fact he'd used her nickname for the first time since they'd *reconnected*—for lack of a better term—she said, "I love bears."

His brows bunched. "Since when?"

"Since...since I started loving bears."

When he smirked, she was sure he recalled the bear viewing tour during their trip to Brooks River Falls in Alaska. It had been fun watching the black bears combing the salmon-filled river and belly-flopping in the water. But when a brown bear had walked right onto the porch of the cabin they'd been staying in and practically knocked on the door, she'd freaked out.

Rolling her eyes away from an amused Nico, she stared at the TV, paying little attention to what was happening on the screen. She could feel Nico's probing eyes on her; it was like a gentle caress teasing her skin.

Nico broke their lingering silence. "I'm sorry about your father."

Gadiya tensed at the mention of Silas Lassiter. His death a little over a year ago still haunted her. Never peeling her eyes away from the screen, she said, "Thank you. I thought you would have been there. He loved you like a son. Still talked about you all the time."

"Even after I broke his little girl's heart?"

"Yep, even after that," she said in a low tone.

Her father used to tell her often Nico had a good reason for leaving, that a man who truly loved a woman didn't simply up and leave without one. He'd said Nico was either protecting or sparing her. Obviously, they'd had two different views of the situation.

"Gadi, I—"

"Let's not, Nico."

Gadiya made a move to leave the bed, but Nico captured her arm. "I'm sorry. Don't go. I'm enjoying your company. I'm actually feeling a lot better. I think you're magic or something. Like an angel or a fairy. Or a fairy with angel wings."

Gadiya shook her head. "You still have that ridiculous sense of humor."

"Some things never change."

"While others do."

They eyed each other for a long, awkward moment, both obviously trying to read each other's thoughts.

Nico's eyes lowered to her mouth. Heat rose from her stomach to her cheeks.

"Can we watch something else?" His gaze rose. "Please."

Foolishly choosing to stay, she said, "No."

"Still a remote hog, I see."

"I'm a guest."

"You've never been a guest in this house a day in your life."

He was right. Growing up, it had been like her second home. She'd spent far more time here than at her own house. Wherever Phoenix was, you'd find her. And Phoenix was always here. "I can almost smell your mom's chocolate chip cookies."

"Hers were good, but they were never better than yours. Which is kinda odd since she's the one who taught you how to make them."

Gadiya was ten when her own mother died of a brain aneurysm. Mrs. Dupree had become like a second mother to her. And when Mrs. Dupree died several years later, Gadiya had felt the loss just as severely as Nico. They'd had each other to help one another through. It had always been that way. Until Phoenix's death.

"I miss her," said Nico.

"So do I. I don't think we ever stop missing the people we've loved and lost." She kicked herself for how the comment must have sound, like she was admitting to missing him. In an attempt to clean up her statement, she said, "Most of the time that's the case. Not always."

"I'd venture to say it was more often than not."

She didn't miss the implication in his words, and she was sure he knew it.

Nico grinned. "Do you remember the time Mom found us in the storage space under the stairs?"

"God, yes. A minute earlier and she would have gotten an eyeful. You nearly got us in so much trouble."

"*Me*? It was your idea to *explore*."

Their exploring had been her allowing him to stick his hand under her shirt and squeeze twice, and him allowing her to peep inside his underwear with an option to feel. She'd felt.

"I wouldn't have screamed if you hadn't surprised

me with that kiss," she said.

"That was my way of letting you know I wanted you to be my girl. It worked."

Yes, it had. Everyone knew she was Nico Dupree's girl and that no one had better do anything to hurt her. Between Phoenix and Nico, she'd never had to worry about anyone harming her. "It was the worst first kiss ever, by the way."

"I was ten. I got a little better over the years, right?"

A lot better. But she kept that to herself. Refocusing on the television, she said, "Look at that bear slapping the water for salmon."

Again, she could feel Nico's eyes pinned to her. No doubt he knew she was attempting to veer out of memory lane. Being with him was a lot harder than she'd imagined it would be. They shared too much. Too much past, too much pain. She had to get out of there.

"Nico, I—"

"Thank you, Gadiya. I'm not sure I deserve your compassion, but you saw fit to give it to me anyway."

Softening, she said, "I just did what anyone would have done."

"Oh, I doubt that. My mom used to say you had a heart of gold and that I was lucky to have you because young ladies like you were rare. She was right."

"Your mom usually was."

They shared a laugh.

"Yeah, she was." Nico's expression turned serious. "I really needed your company, Gadiya. It's been..." His words trailed off. "I've had some lonely days." He sighed. "Anyway... Thank you for being...you."

Gadiya saw the misery in his eyes. Nico's time away from Mount Pleasance hadn't been all fun and games. He'd gone through something. But what? And why did not knowing bother her so damn much?

6

Nico thought for sure his mind was playing tricks on him, but there was no denying Gadiya's soul-stirring fragrance or her core-warming heat. He wasn't sure when or how she'd ended up in his arms, but he didn't budge a muscle. Mostly in fear of waking her and her pulling away from him.

Judging by the rays of sunlight filtering through the blinds, it was morning. He pieced together the events from the night before. Obviously, they'd both fallen asleep watching TV. Something they'd routinely done in the past. Clearly, that hadn't changed for either of them.

Something else that hadn't changed, Gadiya's wild sleeping habits. While her head was nestled on his outstretched arm, her leg was draped over his body. He tried to fight it, but their entangled limbs stirred him below the waist.

No doubt this would end badly when she woke, but right now, he was going to enjoy every second of having her near. Damn, he'd missed this, waking with Gadiya in his arms. He'd missed her warmth, her scent, her delicate body rousing him.

If he hadn't been convinced before, he certainly was now. Despite what she said, or how she acted, Gadiya still loved him. Well, love might have been a stretch. *Cared*. Definitely cared. It gave him a little glimmer of hope.

By no means was he perfect. He'd made a stupid mistake. Everyone deserved forgiveness. Yeah, even him. Something he'd doubted for a long time. And that uncertainty had contributed to keeping him away from Mount Pleasance. But now he was back and intended to reclaim all he'd lost running from his demons.

His demons.

He couldn't believe he'd almost told her— everything. But something had stopped him.

Nico shifted his head slightly to look down at Gadiya. Even asleep she was gorgeous. His eyes roamed over every inch of her face. *No one can ever love you like I love you. I'm going to make you see that. I'm going to make you love me again.*

As if he'd actually spoken his thoughts aloud, Gadiya moaned, then stirred. He held his breath, praying for at least five more minutes with her in his arms. When she settled, he slowly released the breath he'd been holding.

No, no, no.

He scrunched his nose, then made several more attempts to ward off the sneeze tingling his nose. It didn't work.

The *achoo* sounded like it'd come from a dainty old woman adhering to proper sneeze etiquette during a game of Bridge.

A groggy "Bless you," came from Gadiya.

"Thank you."

In hindsight...

Gadiya bolted upright in the bed and glanced around as if she'd just come out of a twenty-year coma fully alert. Then her head whipped toward him.

Nico flashed a hesitant smile. "Morning." It seemed like the most appropriate thing to say.

"M-morning," she said. "What...?" Her words trailed off as she glanced around the room once more.

When Gadiya's head dipped, he assumed she was checking to see if she was still dressed. "I can make us breakfast," he offered, knowing there was nothing in his fridge but a jug of milk.

"What time is it?"

Nico lifted his cell phone from the nightstand. "Ten." *Ten*? Damn, he couldn't believe he'd slept past six. Apparently, Gadiya's warmth had short-circuited his internal clock. He wasn't sure he'd ever be able to readjust it.

"Shit." Gadiya swung her sexy legs over the side of the bed and hurried to her feet. "I have to go."

"Wait." He came out of the bed after her. Why was she rushing off? It was Saturday. If it was because of her business, he was sure she had people who could operate it efficiently in her absence. Then something less comforting dawned on him. Did she have a man waiting at home for her? "What's the rush?"

She tossed him a look that suggested he already knew the answer. He could assure her he didn't. "Are you rushing home to someone?" It was a risky question, but playing it cautious wouldn't get him anywhere with Gadiya.

She paused her urgent movement. "And if I said yes?"

"Then I'd say that would make my intent a little harder, but not impossible."

Her brow arched. "Your intent?"

Skirting around a response, he said, "Don't let me hold you any longer. Again, thank you for everything. Enjoy your Saturday." Was there really need to elaborate? Gadiya was a smart woman and by no means oblivious. She knew exactly what his intent was.

Both curiosity and protest danced in her stern eyes. Damn, no one could stir his need like this woman. And had he been at full steam, he would have snatched her into his arms and kissed her breathless.

Unfortunately, he didn't have the energy or the speed to dodge the lamp he was sure she'd hurl at him. Gadiya's eyes lowered to his mouth, forcing him to rethink yanking her into his arms. Was it possible she wanted him to kiss her?

Only one way to find out.

Nico took a step closer to her, but before he could capture her mouth, she leveled him with a narrow-eyed warning. He recanted his previous thought. A lamp would surely fly. Falling back, he folded his arms across his chest. "This is fun. This little game we're playing."

"I don't play games, Nico. And I hope you don't think that just because—"

"I don't think anything, Gadiya. You were just being a friend to a friend in need. Wait. Are we friends or enemies? It's all so confusing."

The faintest twitch of a smile tugged at her lips—beautiful, plump lips he desperately wanted to taste. Taste until his own throbbed. *Soon.*

"Have a good day. I'll let myself out," she said, hurrying from the room.

In a whisper, he said, "I'm coming for you, Gadiya. And the only thing your running will accomplish is wearing you out."

***

As hard as she tried, Gadiya couldn't focus on the job Rana had tasked her with. Something as simple as taping off a room to be painted was proving a challenge. She could create an entire forest scene in balloons, but couldn't stick a piece of tape to a wall. She blamed Nico. Damn him for taking up residency in her head and refusing to leave.

How had she allowed herself to fall asleep at his place—especially in a place she shouldn't have been in the first place.

She shouldn't have gone to his house.

The memories had nearly suffocated her.

She shouldn't have entered his room.

The temptation had damn near driven her insane.

And she definitely shouldn't have been in his bed.

Those arms.

Countless times they'd comforted her, held her close, made her feel protected. Snuggled against his warm body had felt so good. Too damn good.

Ugh.

Was she delirious? Had one night in Nico's arms made her forget the hell he'd put her through?

"Gadi!"

Rana's words snapped Gadiya back to reality. Whipping her head toward her sister, she said, "Why are you yelling?"

"Because I've called you three times already. Okay, what is going on with you? You were late for Zumba this morning—which never happens. You've been quiet as a hen in a fox den—which *never* happens. And this is the third time I've caught you staring trance-like at the wall. What is up?"

"I spent the night with Nico," she blurted.

Rana smirked. "Ah, shucks now."

"Nothing happened. Well, a lot happened, but nothing sexual."

"No oral sex?"

"Rana!" Leave it to her sister to believe a man and woman can't lay together without having sex. "I said nothing sexual happened."

Rana flashed a hopeful expression. "Did you kiss?"

"No. There was no touching at all. Well, if you don't count me waking up in his arms."

Rana flashed a confused expression. "I don't understand. You didn't have sex. You didn't kiss. But you woke up in his arms?"

Why was it so hard for Rana to believe things had remained G-rated? "Yes. We talked, and watched TV. I guess I dozed off."

Rana rested her hand on her hip. "When I talked to you yesterday morning, you didn't mention anything about having a date with Nico."

Gadiya sighed. "It wasn't a date."

"Sure sounds like a date to me."

For the next several minutes, Gadiya filled Rana in on the details. From her going to the firehouse to apologize to Nico and the cookies, to him getting horribly sick and blaming her.

Once Rana recovered from her thunderous laughter, she said, "Did you bake laxative cookies? That sounds like something I would do."

"I can't believe you just asked me that. No, I did not." Although, it had briefly crossed her mind, but she would have never done something so vicious. "He looked so..."

"Tempting?"

"Pitiful. I couldn't just bail on him. Despite what may have happened between us in the past, we did love each other once." Gadiya's gaze slid away.

"Aw, Sweetie, please quit doing this to yourself. Quit fighting what you feel for Nico. It's okay to still love him. He was your first true love, and that kind of love seldom dies."

Gadiya fiddled with the spool of tape in her hand. "If Nico ever loved me, how could he just leave like that? He knew how much I loved—" She batted her eyes to disperse the unwanted tears. "I've cried enough over him. I refuse to shed one more tear."

Gadiya recognized the expression on Rana's face.

It was the one that always loudly stated—*I want to say something, but I don't want to hurt your feelings*. She tossed the tape aside. "Say it. Don't worry about it hurting my feelings. I'm a big girl." If she could get over losing Nico, she could surely get beyond whatever Rana needed to say.

"You pushed him away, Gadiya. You pushed us all away. When Phoenix died—"

"Even if that was the case, Rana. You and Sadona stayed. You didn't run off and leave my heart in a thousand pieces. You didn't abandon me. You stayed right by my side, and you helped me through because you loved me."

"Nico loved you, too, Gadiya. He just—"

"Why are you defending him, Rana. You're my sister, not his. You are supposed to be on my side, not his. He's not some golden warrior. He's a coward. When things got rough, he ran. And as far as I'm concerned, he can keep running, because I didn't need him then, and I sure as hell don't need him now."

Gadiya attempted to stomp away, but Rana snagged her arms. As if all of the hurt and pain she'd kept bottled up the past two years had decided to come crashing down on her all at once, Gadiya broke down.

Rana cradled her in her arms and lowered to the floor. "You and Nico have too much unresolved history, Gadi. It's draining you. Until you two face it head-on, neither of you will be able to move forward. With or without each other."

Gadiya rested her head on Rana's lap and closed

her eyes. Rana fingered combed her hair. The move had always had a calming effect. "Every man I've ever loved has left me, Rana. Dad, Phoenix, Nico. I'm a jinx."

Rana tilted her head forward to eye her. "That's not true. Quit saddling yourself with other's burdens. Dad..." Rana sighed. "Dad couldn't handle losing mom, so he turned to the bottle. For years, alcohol was the only way he could cope. And like it does so many, his addiction claimed his life."

Their father had only lived four months after being diagnosed with liver cancer. It had been so hard to watch another man she loved die, but she'd been glad her father was no longer suffering.

"And Phoenix...our brother had fought his demons for so long. Afghanistan changed him. The Phoenix we prayed and cried for when he left was not the Phoenix we got back."

No, he wasn't. She'd known something was different about him—he no longer laughed as much as he had, wasn't as adventurous—but she'd assumed it a side effect of readjusting back into civilian life. "Did Nico know what Phoenix was going through?"

Rana chuckled. "God, no. Phoenix knew Nico told you everything. He swore Sadona and me to secrecy. He didn't want you worrying about him. None of us did. You nearly had a nervous breakdown when he was deployed, remember?"

They both chuckled.

Yeah, she remembered. That had been a sad day and one of the worst days of her life, watching her second best friend head to the front lines of war. "Why couldn't I feel something was wrong, Rana? We were twins. I should have felt his pain."

"Phoenix was good at hiding from the world."

"I could have helped, found him help, stayed by his side every second of the day. Something."

"And that's exactly why he didn't want you to know. He knew you would drain yourself trying to fix it, trying to fix him. Every battle is not yours to fight, baby sister."

Try telling that to her heart.

"Though it's not the way any of us would have preferred, Phoenix found his peace, Gadiya. Now, you have to find yours. With Phoenix's death and with Nico's return."

"I'm trying."

"Seems like to me, you and Nico are fighting the same battle. Survivor's remorse. The three of you were thick as thieves. I think deep down you both blame yourselves for Phoenix's death, but you shouldn't. Neither you nor Nico was responsible for him."

Why did Rana always have to make such perfect sense?

"You and Nico both allowed Phoenix's death to drive a wedge between your relationship. It's sad because you two were so in love once. You've both suffered far more than you should have from his death. He wouldn't have wanted that."

"I miss him," Gadiya said lightly.

"Phoenix or Nico?"

"Both." She couldn't believe she'd just admitted to missing Nico aloud. "I think he's trying to win me back."

"I don't think he ever lost you." Rana jostled Gadiya playfully. "Talk to Nico, Gadi." She placed her hand over Gadiya's heart. "Bare your soul. It's the first step toward happiness."

With sincerity in her tone, Gadiya smiled up at Rana and said, "I love having you as my sister. Thank you for listening and never judging. Thank you for always having my back. Thank you for your sound advice."

"I didn't do anything special. I simply told you what you needed to hear. That's what big sisters do. Whether or not you listen is strictly up to you." Rana winked. "But you're a smart woman. Plus, you know big sister is always right."

"*Always* is a stretch. But I can give you most of the time."

"I'll take it. Now enough lollygagging. I need to whip this money pit into shape. Especially this room. It's going to be ground zero for Bedroom Brushings."

"You finally picked a name. I love it. It sounds so seductive." Perfect for Rana's sensual paintings. Her sister was poetry when she painted. She brought every seductive line she stroked to life on the canvas. Bedroom Brushings was going to be a huge success.

"Thank you." Rana's eyes widened. "Oh. I almost forgot. I have something for you. Stay here. I'll be right back." She raced from the room.

"It better not be another painting of an oversized

penis. You know I'm experiencing a drought, right?"

A short time later Rana returned with a cupcake, a single candle lit in its center. "Congratulations on getting the Fireman's Day contract. That's going to be colossal for The Twisted Balloon. Just remember us little people when you blow up."

Gadiya beamed and accepted the treat. "Lemon with a raspberry compote center?"

"And you know it."

"You spoil me so well. Thank you. Wait. How did you know about the contract?" Especially since she hadn't had the chance to tell anyone.

"I have my sources. And said sources also mentioned that it would not have happened if Nico hadn't stepped forward and agreed to pay the amount your proposal was over budget out of his own pocket."

Gadiya's brow bunched. "He did what?"

Rana passed Gadiya a paint brush. "Sounds like love to me, but you two can discuss that when you talk. We have work to do."

Gadiya snatched the brush. "You can be so complicated sometimes."

"But you love me, nonetheless."

Yes, she did. Gadiya contemplated Rana's words— all of them. Maybe she and Nico did need to have a conversation, but was she prepared?

It didn't matter that her brain said no because her heart said yes.

7

Though Nico had spent most of his life here, some things in Mount Pleasance had changed drastically in the years he'd been gone. He relaxed in the passenger seat as Ollie took him on a tour of several new neighborhoods, a strip mall, and restaurants, all located in a part of town that once housed dilapidated tobacco barns.

At least the square had remained intact, ensuring Mount Pleasance kept that small town feel he'd missed so much during his time in D.C. A smile touched his lips. Damn, he was glad to be home.

His thoughts shifted to Gadiya. How was he going to make her feel his presence?

"That place is a tragedy waiting to happen."

Nico followed Ollie's outstretched hand toward the old cardboard plant that had closed recently. "What's the problem?"

"Vagrants. They've taken up shelter there. With Fall right around the corner, they'll be lighting fires to stay warm. From what I understand there's still a lot of cardboard stored there, which could be a problem.

Ollie was right. This had the potential to be a major problem. One spark and the place could go up in a matter of minutes, trapping only God knows how many inside. Nico massaged the side of his face. "Let's see if we can get the police department to do a sweep, then contact someone at Planning to board the place up. Let them know MPFD will help if need be. I'm sure we can spare a few guys."

"I'll get right on it," Ollie said.

"Thanks." Nico studied the large structure. With a building that size, getting trapped inside would mean certain death if you were unfamiliar with the layout. Add smoke and flames to the equation...it equaled disaster.

"Boss, I gotta ask. Just because...well, just because I'm a little nosey."

Ollie wasn't revealing anything Nico hadn't already picked up on. "What's on your mind, Ollie?"

"You and Gadiya. My girl says you used to be hot and heavy, but that you left her for another woman."

Nico couldn't tell if the last part was a question or statement. Either way, it irked him that someone would start such a vicious and ridiculous rumor. Gadiya had always been the only woman for him and always would be. "What?"

Ollie flashed a palm. "I know, I know. I didn't think that sounded like you, but you just never know." Ollie gave Nico an appraising once over. "One look at you and I knew you were a good brother."

He liked to think so.

Not that it was any of Ollie's business—or anyone else's for that matter—he said, "Gadiya and I dated for a while. Several years, actually. I messed up. But it had nothing to do with another woman.

"Davena—my girl—said you and Gadiya dated like

ten years. You have something against marriage?"

He wasn't the one who had something against marriage. Forever and a day with Gadiya would have been all right with him. "Not me."

"Ah. The old fear of commitment." Ollie shrugged. "Guess women can suffer from it, too."

Nico wasn't sure that was the case at all. "I'm planning on making things right." He hoped Ollie mentioned that to his chatterbox girlfriend, and she'd somehow plant that bug in Gadiya's ear. "Your girlfriend knows Gadiya, huh?" Since Ollie and Davena were transplants to Mount Pleasance, Nico doubted he knew the woman, but she seemed pretty informed about his and Gadiya's business.

"She attends the Zumba class Gadiya teaches over at the old elementary school."

"Zumba? That's that dancing exercise class, right?"

"Yep. I hear Gadiya's real good, too."

That explained her beautiful body. The idea of Gadiya teaching an exercise class tickled him. When they were together, he couldn't get her off the couch for a walk around town without promising her they'd stop at the ice cream shop. "Huh. When exactly are these classes?"

By the sly smirk on Ollie's face, Ollie knew precisely why Nico was asking.

"Tuesday and Thursday evenings at six. Saturday morning at ten."

Saturday mornings at ten. That explained why she'd rushed off the other day. Not for another man, but for her class. A sense of relief rushed over him.

Nico set his focus back out the window. *Zumba*. He wasn't much of a dancer but was in pretty good shape. He could certainly handle an exercise class where all you did was dance. *Zumba*, he repeated to himself. Sounded like a perfect way to spend his Thursday evening.

Several hours later, Nico found himself wandering the halls of Mount Pleasance Elementary. Making his way into the gymnasium, he stopped when he spotted Gadiya bent at the waist, rummaging through a duffle-type bag. He envied those black stretchy pants she wore with such finesse.

An image of him palming her round ass right before driving himself deep inside of her played in his head. The idea caused a tightening in his gut that traveled lower. Shaking off his yearning, he continued moving toward her. Not wanting to startle her, he announced his arrival. "Hey."

She jolted, then turned with urgency. Confusion danced on her face. "Nico? She glanced past him as if expecting to see someone else. "What are you doing here?"

For you, he wanted to say, but instead, said, "I heard Zumba classes were being offered." He glided his hand over his mid-section. "I'm getting a little soft. Thought it was time to step up the cardio."

Gadiya's eyes burned a slow line down his torso. He thought he saw just a hint of admiration in her expression. Maybe she recalled how she used to plant kisses all over his bare chest. Man, he'd loved that shit.

Finding his eyes again, she said, "I see. Have you ever done Zumba before?"

"Um…no, but how hard can it be, right?"

"Right."

A smirk twitched at the corner of her delicious looking mouth. This worried him.

"Well, welcome. It'll be an experience you won't soon forget."

Really worried him.

Nico studied Gadiya as she moved about. Something about her was different. She seemed kinder, gentler, more welcoming toward him. He liked it.

"We'll start in about fifteen minutes," she said.

"Sounds good. I hope I'm dressed okay."

Gadiya scrutinized the red MPFD T-shirt and black sweat pants he wore. "Fine," she said, then diverted her eyes.

Though Gadiya played it cool, Nico knew she was affected by him just as much as he was affected by her. The fact that she could hardly look at him was proof—at least in his mind. He wasn't sure if the no eye contact thing was good or bad, whether the sight of him repulsed her or enticed her.

He chose to believe he enticed her.

"Do I need to stretch or will we do that as a class?" he asked

"We'll do it as a class, but if you want to do it now, you can."

"Nah. I'll wait."

"Okay."

Unable to fight the urge, his eyes lowered to her lime green racerback tank top. Her breasts caused the word ZUMBA printed across the front in turquoise letters to stand out. Remembering how her taut nipples had felt between his lips intensified the heat in his groin. Unconsciously, his tongue glided across his bottom lips. Soon, he assured himself. Soon.

Gadiya cleared her throat, obviously catching him drooling over her breasts. Applying forced decorum, he slid his gaze elsewhere. "Um...is it a big class?"

Gadiya pinned him with accusing eyes but didn't call him out. "About ten. I hope you don't mind being in the class with all women. We typically don't get much male participation."

"You know I'm not camera-shy."

The string of words conjured a memory he really could have done without at the moment. It was the time he'd allowed her to take a few nude shots of him. When she'd gone into her darkroom to process them, he'd followed her in, undressed her, and made love to her right there on the converted bedroom floor. Soft moans played in his head.

"So, are you still into photography?" he asked.

Before she could answer, the sound of voices drew both their attentions. One by one, women filed into the large space. Nico got a little cautious when several of the women's gazes gobbled him up like a last meal.

"You're the new fire chief, right?"

Nico recognized the inquiring woman from the

picture Ollie had proudly shown him. "Yes, I am. And you're Davena." The woman seemed surprised he knew her. "Ollie talks about you all the time."

She nodded and flashed a smile almost as bright as her blonde hair she wore in a small afro. Not everyone could pull off such a radical hair color, but it worked well with her brown skin.

Extending his hand, Nico said, "Nice meeting you."

Several more introductions were made before Gadiya wrangled the class. "Okay, ladies—and gentleman—let's get this party started."

The attendees erupted in cheers. Clearly, these ladies were ready, and so was he.

Or so he thought.

Twenty minutes into the routine, Nico was sure he'd thrown a few parts out of place. Even dressed in full fireman's gear, he couldn't recall ever sweating this profusely. Places he didn't know were places burned. This was torture, and these crazy women appeared to be enjoying every second of it.

His focus slid to Gadiya, who bounced around like a wild woman hyped up on a ten-day caffeine binge. Where was she getting all of that energy? He was barely managing to stay upright. However, the sight of her breasts bouncing and bottom jiggling gave him life.

"Okay, you guys, ready to ramp things up?"

Ramp things up? If this wasn't ramped up, what the hell was it? The groan that slipped out hadn't been intended for anyone's ears. Of course, the entire class eyed him like a weak link in their chain.

"You okay over there, Chief Dupree?" Gadiya asked.

Oh, he had a feeling she was enjoying this. Conjuring as much enthusiasm as he could, he said, "Perfect. Let's ramp it up." He be damned if he crumbled in front of all of these women. Especially mighty mouth Davena.

The music got even louder, faster and the moves more complicated. Out of curiosity, he wondered if Gadiya would attempt CPR when he dropped dead.

8

Gadiya refused to admit how adorable Nico looked. Like an uncoordinated duckling that had had his wings clipped. The man was still as uncoordinated as a two-legged giraffe. Honestly, she hadn't expected him to last this long. But here he was, still going strong. Well, still going. Strong was subjective.

Watching him struggle to continue, she almost felt guilty for making the class more intense than it usually was on Thursday evenings. With his overconfident attitude about Zumba, he needed to be taught a lesson.

She turned away and chuckled when Nico stumbled over his own feet. He still knew how to make her laugh, even if it was unintentional. By far, this was the best entertainment she'd had all year.

A half hour later, class concluded. Instead of leaving with the others, Nico sprawled on the floor, draped his arm over his forehead, and closed his eyes. His chest heaved up and down as if he couldn't get enough air. Several of the departing women offered their assistance, but he fanned them away.

Poor baby.

When only she and Nico remained in the gym, Gadiya stood over him. His skin glistened under the fluorescent lighting. Even all sweaty and spent, Nico roused her hunger for a man. Her eyes unhurriedly glided down his body, stopping at the thin line of dark, curly hairs. She followed the trial until it disappeared under his waistband.

When her nipples tightened and core pulsed, she forced her eyes away. But it was too late; her body had already worked itself into a frenzy. Though she agreed with Rana—that she and Nico needed to talk—the only thing darting through her mind now was mounting this well-hung stallion and riding him—

"You okay?"

"—all night." Her mouth dropped open. "You'll probably feel this all night. But it wasn't so bad, right?"

He released a sexy laugh that reverberated all through her body. All she could do was surrender to the effects.

"Perhaps I underestimated the stamina I'd need for this class."

The mention of stamina took her thoughts somewhere x-rated. Offering her hand, she helped Nico to his feet. When he was up, he didn't readily release the hold he had on her. For a second, Gadiya thought he'd pull her to him. Would that have been so bad? She answered herself quickly, *Yes!*

Gadiya reclaimed her hand and closed it to prolong the tingle Nico's touch had caused. "You did well for your first time. I didn't expect you to last the entire hour."

"Thank you."

Nico lifted the hem of his shirt and wiped his face. The sight of his ripped abs sent a warm sensation racing up her spine. He'd actually had the audacity to say he was getting soft. Dissolving those lines of pure muscle wouldn't be an easy task.

When he lowered his shirt, Gadiya snapped out of her trance. "You deserve a gold star."

"I was determined. There's no stopping a determined man."

His words felt as if they meant more than what was being said. "That's a good attitude to have, especially if you're working toward something attainable. A few more classes and you'll be a pro."

"Does that mean I'm invited back?"

Gadiya moved to collect her things. "Well, the classes are open to the public, so…"

"I'll be back. Maybe one day soon, my performance will stun you."

With her back still to him, she said, "I'm sure there's little you can say or do at this point that could stun me, Nico."

"Are you sure?"

Why did his words feel like some kind of challenge? Gadiya abandoned what she'd been doing and faced him. "What—?"

"You wore a black dress that fell just below your knees. Your hair was in braids but pulled into a bun on the top of your head. You wore black sunglasses throughout the service. At the gravesite, you were seated between Rana and Sadona. You held onto a single red rose that you hesitated placing on the coffin when it was time. But you finally did."

Gadiya's lips parted, but it was a second or two

before she could speak. "You...you were at my father's funeral?"

He nodded. "I wouldn't have missed it. He'd always been more of a father to me than my own father had ever been. I thought staying out of sight was best. You were already dealing with a lot. I didn't want my presence adding to your stress."

She'd been wrong; he was capable of stunning her. Gadiya folded her arms across her chest. "Why didn't you say hello?" Her tone was low and cautious.

"You know I did the right thing by keeping my distance, Gadi."

Yeah, he was probably right. Standing before Nico, she was so conflicted. Her mind, her body, her heart, her soul. Everything quarreled. Not knowing what to say, and before all of the emotion she felt sent tears spilling from her eyes, she turned away. God, she wanted to hate Nico. That way she wouldn't have to face what she still felt for him, what he still meant to her.

But she couldn't.

Nico was so close to her, she could feel his electrifying heat on her back.

"All I'd wanted to do that day was wrap my arms around you and hold you close, protect you. That's all I want to do now. From the moment I crossed the line into Mount Pleasance. This job is not the only reason I returned, Gadiya."

"Why did it take you so long?" Her voice cracked when she spoke. "It shouldn't have taken you so long."

Gadiya flinched when Nico rested his hands on her waist and guided her back until her back molded against his chest. His strong arms closed around her. His energy, their energy, bordered electrifying. She wasn't sure how much of it she could handle before it short-circuited her system.

"Foolish pride. Overzealous ego. Paralyzing fear. All of it. But I'm here now, and I'm determined."

She replayed his words from earlier in her head: *There's no stopping a determined man.*

"I've missed you so much, Gadiya Lassiter," Nico said against the back of her head. "So much."

Did she tell him how much she'd missed him too? Was it too soon to bare all to him? Or did she continue to play *woman in control*?

"I messed up, Gadi, and I've regretted it every single day of my life. I have no right to ask for your forgiveness...but please, baby, give me another chance. Just one more chance to love you."

Gadiya wiped a tear from her cheek, cursing herself for not being stronger. When Nico rotated her to face him, she could see the sincerity in his eyes. The sight put another chink in her armor.

"We've lost so much, Gadiya. Too much. Haven't we suffered enough?"

Rana popped into her head. She'd posed a similar question. Maybe they had. Maybe it was time she stopped running, allow Nico to catch her and see where this thing led.

Before she could respond, Nico's mouth covered

hers. Impulsively, she wanted to shove him away, declare he'd long lost the privilege of kissing her. Protest mounted; unfortunately, it was only in her spinning head. The hands planted so firmly in his chest—the ones meant to push him away—explored the contour of his solid frame.

Instinctively, her lips parted and she accepted his probing tongue. She'd been kissed, but never how Nico kissed her. Long, hard, satisfying. His kisses had always been that way. *Tasting your soul*, he'd say. If the way he seemed to be trying to swallow her whole was any indication, he still savored the flavor.

One hand held her close, the other he used to cup a breast. The pad of his thumb swiped back and forth over her taut nipple. Aroused to a near embarrassing level, she whimpered. It had been a long time since she'd been touched intimately. Two years if she were keeping count. She needed to be satisfied in a way only Nico could accomplish.

The feel of hardness pressing against her intensified her craving. Every stroke of his tongue supercharged her body. Her pulse quickened, her heart batted against her ribcage, her blood seared through her veins. When he deepened their connection, she moaned against their joined mouths, fully under his control.

Large, powerful hands glided down the side of her body until they rested on her butt, giving it a firm squeeze. Lightning bolts of pleasure shot through her from the simple, yet stimulating, act. Tomorrow regret would probably smother her, but tonight she was only focused on the moment.

Nico pulled his mouth away, and like a fiend she suffered instant symptoms of withdrawal. The look he gave her—dark, demanding, and laden with desire— took her breath away. Without moving his lips, he asked the question. And without having to verbally respond, she gave him her answer—that he could have her right then and there.

Nico's gaze darkened with primal lust, a look that suggested she would leave the gym a highly satisfied woman. But before he could act, the gym door creaked open, and things came to a screeching halt.

Commonsense she'd lacked mere moments earlier kicked in, and Gadiya urgently freed herself from him and took several steps back. Both their gazes settled on a visibly stunned Davena. Of all the people who could have walked in on them, why did it have to be the town gossip?

Recovering, Davena said, "Sorry to interrupt." She flashed a knowing smile. "I forgot my towel."

For the first time, Gadiya noticed the white linen lying in a puddle on the floor. Retrieving it, Davena said a second good night and hurried from the space. Knowing how Davena loved to flap her gums, Gadiya knew by morning the entire town would have heard about what she'd witnessed.

With her brain finally firing on all cylinders, Gadiya took Davena's interruption as a sign. A sign that she and Nico had been moving too fast. Moving on a course she'd been very eager to travel. But now it felt as if they'd been wandering in the wrong direction.

By his yielding expression, Nico recognized the conflict in her eyes. When he rested a hand on the side of her face, she wanted to close her eyes and rub her cheek against it like a cat adoring its human. In silence, they watched each other. Unlike moments earlier, Nico's stare held far more understanding than scorching heat. For that, she was grateful.

A low wattage smile curled his lips, "Good night." And he left.

Could it really be that simple? She'd expected him to grill her, attempt to finish what they'd started, or at least discuss what had brought it to a standstill. Nothing. As he made haste toward the double doors, she couldn't help wondering, *why no fight*.

Fifteen minutes later, Gadiya pulled into Ms. Ethel's driveway. Gripping the steering wheel, she took several deep breaths before exiting. Grabbing her duffle bag, she moved to the porch and rang the bell.

Ms. Ethel's frail voice called out, "Coming."

Gadiya could hear the aging woman's feet shuffle toward the door. The thought of spending the next half hour with the wise woman gave Gadiya a much-needed feeling of relief. Every Thursday after her regular Zumba class, Gadiya traveled across town to Ms. Ethel's for a chair Zumba session, since Ms. Ethel couldn't do the more intense class at the gym.

The door creaked open, and Ms. Ethel peered out. "Hello. Come on in." A look of concern spread across

Ms. Ethel's pecan-toned face. "Are you okay? You seem...troubled."

"Nothing too serious." Lies. All lies. What had happened between her and Nico had been extremely serious. Like nuclear reactor meltdown severe.

"Good, good."

Ms. Ethel stood no more than four feet tall. She'd been a few inches taller before time and osteoporosis had snagged some of her height. The pink T-shirt, white sweat pants, and blue tennis shoes she wore brought a smile to Gadiya's face.

"I see you're ready to work," Gadiya said. "Sorry I'm late. I had an issue at the gym."

Gadiya trailed Ms. Ethel into the family room. Ms. Ethel had already set up her chair in the middle of the floor. Gadiya dropped her bag and rested her hands on her hips. "Young lady, did you drag that chair all the way in here by yourself?"

Ms. Ethel mimicked Gadiya's stance, a little unsteady on her feet. "Yes."

Gadiya bit back a laugh. At eighty-nine, Ms. Ethel was still as feisty as ever. "In the future, will you please wait until I get here and let me move the chair for you?"

"Maybe." Her dark brown eyes twinkled, and a smile curled her purple painted lips. A second later, she pumped her tiny fist into the air. "Let's do this."

And they did.

As usual, after their session, Gadiya took a seat on the antique sofa. She and Ms. Ethel enjoyed tea and gingersnap cookies. Every Thursday, their conversations were typically the same, Ms. Ethel's late husband, Cooper. But Gadiya enjoyed watching how she lit up talking about the man she'd loved a lifetime, as Ms. Ethel put it.

"Cooper was my soul mate. I miss him something awful. Not a day goes by I don't talk to him. And as crazy as it seems, I can feel him listening."

It didn't seem crazy at all. It was true love.

"But enough about me. Every week I hog the conversation. We never talk about your love life."

Or lack of one. "There's nothing to talk about, really. Unlike you, I've never found that one true love. My soul mate." Though, at one point, she'd believed it to be Nico, he'd proved her wrong. "I thought I had, but... I guess it just wasn't meant to be."

Ms. Ethel smiled warmly. "Don't worry. You'll find that special one, get married, and have a houseful of babies."

Gadiya was okay with finding the special one and babies, but the marriage thing... "I'm never getting married." She'd never had the desire, even when she and Nico dated. Thankfully, he'd been okay with that.

"Why on earth not?"

Her thoughts shifted briefly to her parents, then pushed the memories away. "Marriage is just not my thing."

"Lord, you young folk. Well, I'm a wise old bird, so trust me when I say never say never. Love can do some mighty powerful things." Ms. Ethel flashed another warm smile. "It's a shame that handsome fire chief is already attached. You two would make a lovely couple."

Gadiya stiffened. "The *new* fire chief?" As if there was another.

"Yes. I got a visit from him the other day. We talked for about an hour." Ms. Ethel smiled as if it were the best conversation she'd ever had. "He said he was visiting all the elders in town. Wasn't that sweet of him? Unlike that degenerate who held the position before him." Ms. Ethel's face contorted, then relaxed. "Lord, he's as handsome as one of those men you see modeling clothes in the magazine. Reminds me of my Cooper. Handsome and devoted."

Gadiya's heart plummeted. If Nico was already attached, why had he kissed her? Anger started to swell. What kind of game was he playing?

"That fire chief is a fellow any woman could love. Pleasant, kindhearted, chivalrous. You just don't see that nowadays. She's a lucky woman, whoever she is. Told me he's loved her since he was eight years old."

Ms. Ethel's words jerked Gadiya from her thoughts.

"I'm not sure an eight-year-old really knows what love is, but he convinced me." Ms. Ethel laughed. "Called her his honeycrisp because she loves those mammoth-sized apples. They are good, but a little too tart for me."

Gadiya's lips parted, but nothing came out. *Honeycrisp.* That was what Nico used to call her. The story he'd told Ms. Ethel had been about her. Since Nico hadn't used her name, Gadiya found no need to reveal their history together. At least not until she figured out what the hell to do about Nico.

"I know his mother would have been so proud to see the man he's become." Ms. Ethel shook her head. "Sad, just so sad."

Fumbling past her thoughts, Gadiya said, "You knew the fire chief's mother?"

"No, but I knew his grandmother very well. Back in Kinnard where Cooper and I used to live, Irene and I used to do charity work together." Ms. Ethel shook her head again. "She took her daughter's death hard. Such a shame a pretty thing like that would end her own life over that no-count husband."

Gadiya's brow furrowed. They must have been talking about two different people. Nico's mother had died of a heart attack in her sleep. Everyone knew that.

"Somehow it was arranged that the body be moved from Mount Pleasance to Kinnard. My Cooper performed the autopsy," she said with pride. "Oh, how he'd regretted falsifying the cause of death. Said it went against everything he believed in. Guess we all have made poor choices at one time or another. That one haunted him to the grave."

The air in the room grew thick, and Gadiya found it hard to breathe. *Mrs. Dupree*— She swallowed hard. Had Mrs. Dupree taken her own life? Was it possible?

"Lord, I probably shouldn't be telling you any of this. Please don't mention it to anyone. Even with all the time that has passed, I imagine this could still do irreparable damage."

"I won't," Gadiya said absently, her thoughts swirling like the blades of a windmill during high winds. Could this really be true? "Who knew about this, Ms. Ethel? About how Mrs. Dupree died?"

"Well, let's see." The woman rested her thin index finger against her chin and glanced heavenward. "Me, of course, Irene and Lonni, and that despicable cheat of a husband of hers."

"Did Ni—" Gadiya stopped abruptly. "Did the fire chief know what had really happened to his mother?" Gadiya prayed the woman said no.

"Hmm. Yes. Yes, I believe he did."

Oh, God.

Ms. Ethel snapped her fingers. "In fact, I know he did, because I recall Irene breaking down as she told me how her grandson blamed himself for his mother's death. Poor fellow had taken it so hard." She shook her head. "Suicide, it's so—" She paused. "Dear, God. Where is my brain?" Ms. Ethel rested a delicate hand on Gadiya's arm. "I'm so sorry if I dredged up painful memories. Sometimes my mouth moves before my brain even knows I'm talking."

"It's okay," Gadiya assured the troubled woman. "I have to go, Ms. Ethel. I'll see you next week."

"Oh. Okay. Would you like to take some cookies with you?"

"No, ma'am." Gadiya gathered her things and hurried to the door.

"Thank you," Ms. Ethel called out, but Gadiya didn't respond.

Inside the vehicle, Gadiya felt as if she were having a panic attack. What she'd just learned overwhelmed her. So much made sense now.

9

The sound of the doorbell jolted Nico out of slumber.
When he'd gotten home from Zumba, he'd face-planted
onto the couch, where he still remained. If she were still
alive, his mother would have scolded him for soiling the
couch in his sweaty clothes.

Focusing his eyes, he checked his watch. It was
passed ten. Who would be visiting this late in the
evening? And on a weekday?

Making a motion to move, he grunted from the
discomfort that radiated throughout his entire body.
Shit. He hadn't experienced this much ache when
Gadiya pushed him out of a tree when they were
younger. His mother had labeled it a love tap, despite
her not knowing his strong feelings for Gadiya back
then.

Gadiya and his mother.

Two women he'd loved more than anything on
earth. Both women he'd lost by stupid decisions he'd
made.

The euphoric feeling he experienced remembering
his and Gadiya's kiss served as a pain reliever for the
past. In the far-too-short time their mouths had been
joined, she'd awakened something dormant in him. His
want for her had morphed into desperate need inside
the gym. And he'd worn one painful as hell erection to
prove it.

How in the hell had things gone from sweltering hot to frozen so fast?

No doubt in his mind she'd wanted him just as bad as he'd wanted her. But after Davena's untimely intrusion, he no longer saw desire in Gadiya's eyes; he'd only seen pleading. And as much as he wanted to ignore it, he couldn't. She'd been battling something—uncertainty, fear—he didn't know. All he knew was that she was the only one who could slay it.

Hobbling to the door, he cursed whoever stood on the opposite side, forcing him to use energy he didn't have. When he yanked the door open, Gadiya's presence struck him like a cannonball to the gut.

The exhausted expression on her face troubled him, and with just one look into her red, puffy eyes, he knew she'd been crying. Alarmed, he said, "Gadiya, what's wrong?" If someone had hurt her, he'd kill them with his bare hands.

"For two years I've allowed myself to hate you, Nico. For two years I've cursed your name, cursed your memory." She paused, her eyes clouding with tears. "I never once considered your leaving had nothing to do with me at all."

Nico eyed her curiously. Though she was right, he wasn't sure where any of this was coming from—or going. Deep down, something told him he wouldn't like either when he found out.

A single tear trailed down her cheek. "I know, Nico. I know about Mama Dupree."

Nico's body tensed. His lips parted, but no words

readily escaped. He stared at her a moment. How could she know? Not wanting to tip his hand—in case they were talking about two entirely different things, he said, "What do you *think* you know, Gadiya?"

Gadiya's tone was warm when she said, "I know her death was not caused by a heart attack, Nico. I know she kil—"

"Stop!" His tone softened. "Just stop." He didn't need to be reminded of how his mother had died, or the role he'd played in her death. He swallowed hard, emotions he didn't want to experience swirling out of control inside him.

Without another word, he turned and walked away. Gadiya trailed him. He lowered himself to the couch, rested his elbows on his thighs, and lowered his head. He'd known eventually he'd have to tell Gadiya about his mother, it was the only way she'd fully understand why Phoenix taking his own life had hit him so hard, why he'd run, but he wasn't ready to do it now. After all of these years, it was still a painful subject.

Gadiya eased down next to him. "You were weathering your own storm. I never saw past my own hurt and pain to recognize yours. To recognize what dreadful memories Phoenix's death brought back for you."

If she only knew the half of it.

"Nico, I was so selfish. I made everything about me. I never considered there was a deeper reason why you left. I just thought you'd stopped loving me or that there was another woman."

His head rose, and he eyed Gadiya. "You really think I could ever stop loving you? I've loved you since we were kids." His face contorted. "Another woman? Honestly, Gadiya?"

She shrugged. "What else was I supposed to think, Nico. You just...left. I needed you, but now I know you needed me, too. I wasn't there for you. I'm so sorry."

"I love that about you. That need to always save the world and everyone in it. Don't put this on yourself, Gadi. This was all on me."

"We shared *everything*, Nico. Why didn't you talk to me? Tell me what you were going through."

In a reserved tone packed with sentiment, he said, "How, Gadiya? I didn't want to compound your grief by adding mine to it. When Phoenix died, you shut down. You shut me out."

She dragged a hand across her cheek. "I never meant to alienate you."

"I know it wasn't intentional." He turned away again, the urge to pull her into his arms was too great. If he grabbed her, he wouldn't let her go this time. "Phoenix's death put us both in a bad place. I felt as if I were doing more damage to you than good. I couldn't be what you needed at the time. I thought leaving was for the best." He chuckled. "I...I...I... Sounds like we were both selfish as hell."

"Yeah, it does."

When Gadiya stood, he assumed she was about to flee from him. Instead, she moved to the mantle, lifted a picture of his mother, and studied it.

In time, he would tell her everything about his mother's death; she deserved that much.

With her back to him, Gadiya said, "You were right at the gym. We have suffered enough."

He stood, but didn't move toward her, wanting to maintain the distance she'd placed between them. "What are you saying?"

Gadiya replaced the frame. With her back still to him, she said, "I see now that your leaving was less about us and more about the memories and pain Phoenix's death triggered. I sympathize with you, Nico. Truly, I do. But it doesn't alter the fact that you *chose* to leave, that you *chose* to shatter my heart."

Though she was right, Nico didn't like the sound of it. Taking one step closer, he said, "Look me in the eyes and tell me you don't still love me, Gadiya. If you can do that...I'll let you go. I'll never bother you again. But you have to look me in the eyes and make me believe there's no hope for us."

Gadiya finally faced him. "I can't."

"Then give me another chance. I need you, Gadiya."

She brushed past him but stopped before reaching the door. Not bothering to face him, she said, "If you need me like you say you do, you're going to have to work for me, Nico. Work for my heart. Work for my love. And if—or when—I feel you deserve them...I'll be yours."

Before he could respond, Gadiya continued to make haste toward the door. Oh, no. He wasn't allowing her to get away that easily, not without adding his own fuel to the flames. This was a challenge he intended to satisfy, and she needed to know that. "Gadiya?"

She stopped and shifted her head toward him. "Yes?"

"You don't stand a chance. I'm coming for you with everything I've got. And baby...I've got a whole lot. You're already mine, Gadi, and you know it. But I will give you that reason to love me again."

A lazy smile touched her lips. "We'll see."

That they would.

***

Gadiya eyed Nico behind the steering wheel in a thin, navy blue long-sleeved tee and dark jeans. Lord, he was all types of handsome and sinfully pleasing on the eyes. When he'd asked her on a date mere hours after her letting him know there just might still be a chance for them, she'd accepted. Her lack of hesitation had stunned her. Nico, too, if his lingering pause after she'd said yes had been any indication.

He'd wasted no time on his *winning her heart* mission, which told her he was serious about them. So was she.

Nico turned toward her. "What?"

"What, what?"

"You keep stealing glances at me. Are you assessing my rugged good looks?"

A sexy smile curled his lips. Yes, she was. Of course, she didn't confess it. That wasn't the only thing she'd been doing. She'd been considering how happy she was to be here with him. Of all places she could have been on a Saturday morning—including her canceled Zumba class—she was glad she was there is Nico.

Did that make her stupid? Naïve? Both?

If so, she didn't care.

"Just drive," she said.

Gadiya did the calculations in her head. It had been six months since she'd gone on a real date. That's if you could even call that calamity a date. *Note to self: never, ever, ever allow your free-spirited sister to talk you into joining another online dating site.*

Jonah. The name was sour in her thoughts. The plastic surgeon had seemed sane enough in his profile. And on paper, he was a catch. But an hour into the date, she'd been ready to toss him into the recycle bin.

What paper hadn't mentioned was Dr. Jonah Wells' obsession with sex. Every other comment he'd made had dripped with sexual innuendo he'd thought was humorous. Gadiya had found it tacky and repulsive.

He'd been late picking her up, had talked about himself most of the evening, and had some obvious affliction to opening doors for women. As if that hadn't been bad enough, he'd assumed a trip to a dollar-fifty movie and a mediocre dinner would have been sufficient enough to get him laid.

She ground her teeth remembering how he'd

called her a tease and had stormed off her porch muttering something that sounded like *you're probably a sorry lay anyway.*

Ha.

Sorry lay? She would have had him begging for more.

"What's that look for?"

Nico's words plucked Gadiya from her thoughts.

"What look?" she asked.

"You had a disgusted expression on your face."

Had she really? "I was just thinking about something."

"With that look, I hope it didn't involve me."

"No. The last date I—" She stopped abruptly. "No, it had nothing to do with you."

"Must have been a really bad date," he said dryly.

Gadiya eyed him a moment, his expression suggesting the fact she'd dated troubled him. Hadn't he dated? She was sure he'd had no trouble finding a willing bed partner. The idea of him touching, kissing, teasing, making love to another woman infuriated her. "It was. Where'd you say we were going again?"

"Have you dated a lot since we...?" His words trailed off.

Obviously, he hadn't picked up on her attempt to change the subject. Or maybe he had but chose to ignore it. "No." It was an honest answer. After Colton Chesapeake, then the doctor debacle, she'd taken a dating hiatus.

Gadiya didn't bother asking Nico about his dating

track record. She had no desire to hear about the women who'd occupied his time.

"You've been awfully quiet for most of the ride. You're either uncomfortable or regret being here with me. Which is it?" Nico said.

"You, of all people, should know I don't do anything I don't want to do. If I'm here, it's because I want to be."

"Good."

When his eyes lowered to her mouth, she actually wanted him to lean over and kiss her as he had in the gym. How pathetic. She hadn't been in the vehicle with the man an hour and was already lusting after him.

This is going to be a long day.

Pulling her gaze away before she overheated, she said, "Are we almost to wherever we're going?"

"Another twenty minutes or so."

A short time later, they entered Ann Orchard. Now she understood why Nico had told her to dress comfortably and to wear tennis shoes. They were going apple picking. She didn't want to show it, but she was as giddy as a five-year-old who'd just gotten a new bike.

"Are you okay with picking some apples?" Nico asked, a knowing smile on his face.

Yes! She shrugged nonchalantly. "Yeah, I guess."

Nico chuckled before exiting the truck and moving to her side to open the door. Offering his hand, he guided her down onto the uneven earth. A misstep slammed her into Nico's chest. His arms closed around her as if she'd intentionally nestled her body against his.

She sent her brain the command to pull away, but the defiant organ refused to process it. Taking in a lungful of Nico's manly scent, she caught herself before she moaned with delight. Enjoying a few more seconds of his solidness, she reared back. "Thank you."

For a moment, she didn't think he would let her go, but his arms finally fell away. Truthfully, she wouldn't have minded him holding onto her for a while longer.

As they moved along the gravel trail toward the entrance, Nico said, "I'm glad you said yes, Gadiya."

As if her heart had given her any other option. "Me, too."

While Nico stood in the long line to purchase tickets for the hayride, Gadiya explored. They couldn't have had a more ideal day for apple picking. Sunny and not a cloud in the sky. And despite it being only a few weeks until Fall, the temperature was a comfortable eighty degrees with a gentle breeze.

Reading the display board, she discovered there were over twenty varieties of apples available for picking, some she'd heard of, some she hadn't. Honeycrisp was third on the list. "Before you leave, be sure to visit the country store and sample one of our apple cider donuts," she mumbled to herself, reading the information board.

Apple cider donuts? Hmmm.

The apple cider, apple salsa, and apple butter didn't sound too bad either.

"There you are."

Gadiya turned to see Nico approaching, a brilliant smile on his face. Looking past him, she spotted two women openly drooling over him. A ping of jealousy prickled her skin. Then she told herself how silly she was being. "That was quick."

"They opened another line. You ready?"

She nodded.

There were so many people aboard the hay-strewn, tractor-pulled trailer that Gadiya was practically in Nico's lap. He draped an arm around her shoulder as if it were as normal as breathing. She tensed, then relaxed. Inwardly, she denied how much she actually liked the feeling of his arm around her. Her stirring body obviously appreciated it, too.

Nico glanced at the apple harvest schedule he'd been given. "Would you look at that? Honeycrisp apples." He smirked.

Gadiya's eyes lowered to Nico's mouth, so close she could practically feel his breath feather her skin. And as if he'd known she'd wanted him to kiss her, he did. It wasn't the long, lingering, soul-stirring kiss she craved; it was a quick and gentle peck. One that preempted to there being more where that one had come from, if she wanted them.

Oh, she did.

Gadiya touched her lips. "Why did you do that?"

Close to her ear, he whispered, "Because I wanted to. Because I needed to. Because you wanted me to. And you know you liked it."

"Is that your girlfriend?"

The tiny voice drew both Gadiya and Nico's attention to the child directly across from them. His bright, green eyes twinkled as he covered his mouth and snickered.

"*Hunter!*" his mother—or whom Gadiya took to be his mother—said with warning, then apologized profusely, her cheeks fiery with assumed embarrassment.

"Yes, she is my girlfriend," Nico said.

Gadiya whipped her head toward him.

In a quiet tone, he said, "You better turn away before I kiss you again. And this time it won't be quick or innocent."

In true Lassiter woman form, she'd started to call his bluff, until the glimmer in his eye told her if his lips touched hers again, she'd be in big trouble.

Hunter spoke again, "I have a girlfriend, too. Her name is Toya."

Playfully rolling her eyes away from a triumphant-looking Nico, she set her gaze on Hunter again. Nico simply laughed and further roused the talkative boy.

"Oh, yeah? Is she as pretty as my girl?" Nico asked.

Hunter shook his head with urgency. "No, but she's pretty enough for me."

This garnered laughs all around them. A child made life appear so simple.

Several minutes later, they filed off the trailer and made their way into the orchard. The sight of all of those honeycrisp apples just dangling for her to claim brought a wide smile to her face.

Moving to one of the numerous trees, she examined a piece of fruit before plucking it off the limb. She wanted to bite right into it, but they'd been warned not to indulge until the fruit had been properly washed.

"Would you like for me to carry your basket for you?" Nico asked.

She passed it to him. Before long, it would be a heavy nuisance. Scrutinizing more apples, she said, "Why did you tell Hunter I was your girlfriend?"

"Who?"

She slid a narrow-eyed gaze at him.

"Oh, that Hunter. You're a girl, and we're friends, right?" Obviously, he found her *I'm about to strangle you* look amusing because he laughed. "Okay, okay. I'm sorry. I should have never said that."

"And the arm around my shoulders?"

"You know how impulsive I can sometimes be. I'm sorry."

Something told her he was anything but. Her attention slid back to the tree. "The kiss?"

"*That* I'm not sorry about. I enjoyed it very much."

Never making eye contact with him, she said, "Well, you can't just go around kissing people when the mood strikes."

"I'm not kissing *people*. I'm kissing you." He plucked a leaf from one of the apples and brushed the side of her face with it. "And I intend to keep kissing you. And kissing you. And kissing you."

Gadiya tossed an apple into the basket, folded her arms across her chest, and cocked a combative brow.

"Oh, really."

An overly confident Nico flashed a brilliant smile that drew her attention to his delectable mouth.

Dang it. Stop that.

"Absolutely."

His gaze darkened, causing a warm sensation in her stomach.

"I'm working for your heart, remember? Tender kisses are all a part of my strategy." He smirked and ventured to another tree.

"Oh, yeah. Well...well...your strategy sucks. How about that." She wanted to add, *just like your kisses*, but that would have been a lie.

10

Nico and Gadiya arrived back at her place a little after ten that evening. A full day of apple picking had left her pooped. Who knew such an enjoyable task could be so exhausting. Like a true southern gentleman, Nico walked her to her front door, signaling the end to their second first date.

"Here you are. Safe and sound," Nico said, brushing a hair behind her ear, then swiping a finger along her jawline.

"I had a great time, Nico." Which was no exaggeration. "Thank you."

"So did I. And you're very welcome. I look forward to doing this again. Soon."

Soon worked for her.

A moment of sexually-charged silence played between them. She wanted to invite him inside. Take it slow, she reminded herself.

Gadiya hoped her taut nipples weren't showing through the pink tee she wore. When Nico's eyes lowered to her breasts, she had her answer. A faint sound rumbled in his chest.

Finding her eyes again, he said, "I guess we should say good night."

Fishing the key from her purse, she popped the lock and stepped inside before Nico further clouded her good judgment. "Good night, Nico. Safe travels."

Before the door completely closed, Nico snaked his foot inside. Pulling it open again, she said, "Did you want something?" God, had she really just asked that? The twinkle in his eye answered for him.

Nico stepped inside the threshold and leaned against the door jamb. His perfect, commanding, so-in-her-face body emitted a wave of heat that nearly seared her. "Y-yes, Nico? Did you want to say something?"

"I'm not trying to get out of hard work. In fact, I plan to work my ass off for you, woman. And I *will* conquer your heart."

A powerful urge blossomed inside her, one that tempted her to reach out and touch him just to satisfy the need of her aching fingers. Somehow, she managed to elude the ravenous need and form a sentence. "Why are you telling me this?"

"To say that not only do I intend to conquer your heart, I plan to conquer your body, as well."

A bout of nerves shook her. For a long, strained moment, all she could do was stare. Nico's expression remained like steel. If his claim had been meant to rattle her, he'd succeeded. Finally, locating her words in her frazzled brain, she said, "And I'm supposed to just fall into bed with you?"

"No. I actually had envisioned scooping you into my arms, carrying you to the bedroom, and placing you down gently." He rubbed two fingers across his bottom lip and narrowed his eyes. "That's probably the only gentle thing that'll take place."

"I..." Gadiya swallowed hard. "I see. And I'm

assuming you're hoping I'd invite you in to do all of those things."

"That would be good. Great, actually."

"Uh-huh. And if I said no?" He released a single sexy chuckle that sent ripples of pleasure to her soul.

He shrugged one shoulder. "In that case, I guess I'll have to continue longing to touch you, taste you, make love to you. And you'll have to continue to fantasize about having me deep inside of you."

Her eyes widened. "I'm not—"

"*Gadi...*" he said in a drawn out, accusing tone. "You can't lie to me. I can feel your desire every time you look at me, every time we're this close to one another."

What in the hell type of vibes was her defiant, disloyal body sending off to this obviously vigilant man? Nico continued, raising her heart rate with every bold word spoken.

"It's been a long time, but I can still read your body. It's a language I'm fluent in, one I'll never forget."

Funny, she didn't remember him being so damn arrogant.

"Undoubtedly, you know I want you. Want you more than any man should want anything in this lifetime. Luckily, I'm a patient man. But just know that every second I go without you is a second I'm going to reclaim in the most fervent manner conceivable."

Gadiya gnawed at the corner of her lip. A corner of Nico's mouth lifted into a wicked grin. After placing a kiss on her cheek, he was gone.

Closing the door, Gadiya heaved several deep breaths. She popped the lock before she ran after Nico and dragged him inside. Resting her hand over her fluttering stomach, she wrangled her frayed nerves. If a declaration, mere words, could arouse her like this, what would happen when Nico followed through?

Escaping to the bathroom, she splashed her face with cold water, then stared at herself in the mirror. "That was close."

She gave herself and imaginary high-five for resisting temptation. Unfortunately, she wasn't sure she actually had anything to celebrate. Nico had declared war, and she wasn't sure if— No, she was sure, very sure, very, very sure that she was not prepared to engage in his type of warfare.

***

Slumped on the couch, Nico flicked through station after station. Over three hundred channels and there was nothing on television he wanted to watch. What he would have loved for his eyes to be trained on at this late hour—midnight, he noted—was Gadiya, sound asleep in his arms. But she'd blocked that programming several hours ago.

Why in the hell was she playing this game with him? They both knew where their relationship was headed. Happily ever after, he told himself. But first, they apparently needed a stint in *Figuring-shit-out*, USA.

Truthfully, she was the only one who needed to

sort out her feelings. He knew exactly what he wanted. He wanted her, in every dirty, nasty, beautiful sense of the word.

When headlights danced on his ceiling, as if someone had pulled into his driveway, he sat forward. The sound of a car door closing pulled him to his feet. Peeping through the blinds, he experienced an intense sensation.

Nico had the door open by the time Gadiya made it onto the porch. He scanned her from head to toe, confused by the brown trench-style coat she wore. There was a nip in the air, but it wasn't cold enough for this type of apparel just yet.

Ignoring the clothing, his eyes climbed Gadiya's frame. Her gentle fragrance of something sweet and flowery wafted through the air. Despite his efforts, an erection swelled. He made a vow: Gadiya was not escaping again. If he didn't have her, he'd lose his damn mind.

"I...um...had a dream about you," she said instead of a customary greeting. "It was...detailed," she continued.

Sexual, he silently translated.

"After that, I couldn't fall back asleep." She fiddled with the belt of her coat. "I know it's late, but I thought...I don't know, maybe, you'd want to watch TV or something."

It was the *or something* that intrigued him.

Gadiya released a strained sigh. "The entire ride over I tried to convince myself that it was too soon to forget what happened between us, that it was too soon to forgive you..."

"But you're here. And you don't do anything you don't want to do," he reminded her.

"I'm here because I want to be."

And he was damn glad she was.

Curious, he grabbed one of the ends of the belt holding her coat together and yanked on it. When it fell open, it revealed Gadiya wasn't wearing anything underneath but a pair of silky, fire engine red panties. His favorite color. His favorite way of seeing her body—bare.

"Why fight the inevitable?" she said.

The sight before him caused his dick to throb. He wanted to shout, cheer, pump his fist in the air, but played it cool. Taking her hand, he led her inside, closed the door, and pinned her against it.

He stared at her long and hard, never making a move. Then he saw it...her absolute surrender.

Crashing his mouth to Gadiya's, he kissed her as if it would be the last time he would be allowed to taste her like this. Hell, for all he knew, it would be. And if that just so happened to be the case—which he strongly doubted—he'd make sure she remembered this moment.

Their tongues sparred, taunted, teased...claimed, danced, harmonized. He hungrily explored every inch of her mouth as if making up for all the time that had been lost. His hands—shaky with anticipation—roamed over her warm, soft skin, touching everywhere.

Cupping her ample breasts, he glided his thumbs lightly across her budded nipples. A deep moan rumbled in Gadiya's throat. Moving his hand further up her body, he brushed the coat off her shoulders, allowing it to fall into a puddle at their feet.

When he finally found the willpower to pull away, Gadiya's mouth searched for his. He pecked her gently. "Don't worry, I'll be back."

He peppered kisses along her jaw, down the column of her neck, across her shoulder, and to her breasts. Taking a hardened nipple into his mouth, he sucked it gently. This time, a series of moans escaped from Gadiya.

The sweet sound was music to his ears. He'd missed her sexual melody, missed making her squirm under his delicious torture, missed the way her hands roamed over his body when they were in the throes of passion.

With a bent finger, he played with her clit through the damp fabric of her underwear. The idea that he'd made her so wet further roused his already hellacious hunger for her.

Gadiya ground herself against his knuckle. "Nico...please."

The fact she was begging for this drove him absolutely insane, but it didn't alter his strategy. It had been so long since he'd been here with Gadiya, and he intended to savor every second, every inch of her.

"You'll get all of me tonight, baby, don't worry." But he would take his time giving it to her.

Nico applied more pressure to her sensitive spot and she whimpered. This moment had played in his head a thousand times over the years they'd been apart, even more when he'd returned. He'd be damned if he rushed it. Gadiya would experience all of his passion. All twenty-four bottled up months of it.

She'd feel it through his lips.

She'd feel it through his tongue.

She'd feel it through his fingers.

She'd feel it the second he entered her.

Oh, she would definitely feel it when he buried himself inside of her.

His throbbing manhood twitched at the promise.

Coming to his full height, Nico scooped Gadiya into his arms and headed toward the bedroom, but stopped before he'd made it there.

Concern danced in Gadiya's weak eyes. "What's wrong?"

"Other than the fact I can't make it another step without tasting you, nothing." Placing her on the wooden console table in the hallway, he lowered to his knees, removed her panties, and feasted on her like a man food deprived.

Gadiya cried out, her hands gripping the edge of the table so tightly, her knuckles cracked. He spread her wet lips further apart and suckled her clit. Holding her open with one hand, he used the other to curl two fingers inside her.

"Right there, Nico. Oh God, right there."

After one or two more flicks of his tongue, Gadiya

came undone. Her muscles contracted against his coated fingers, but he continued gliding them in and out of her. For a brief moment, he thought she'd buck off the table. If anyone were within several feet of his house, they'd swear he was killing her.

When Gadiya finally settled, he kissed his way up her body. "You taste better than I remember."

Claiming her mouth, he hummed with satisfaction. Unlike earlier, this kiss was untamed and raw. He hoisted her into his arms, her legs wrapping around him. Tasting her had been an excellent introduction, but he was far from done with reacquainting himself with her body.

They had a whole lot of passion-filled moments to make up for. And he planned to get through at least half of them tonight.

11

When Nico hoisted her into his arms, Gadiya wasn't sure where she'd gotten the energy to wrap her legs around him. That intense orgasm had left her feeling like she'd taught ten Zumba classes back to back, but she wanted more. And he seemed poised to give it to her.

In silence, Nico carried her the remainder of the way to his bedroom. How did she ever believe her heart could stop beating for this man? She cradled his face between her hands and kissed him gently. "I never slept with him," she said.

Nico's brow furrowed and he stopped shy of entering the room. "You never slept with whom?"

"Colton Chesapeake. I never slept with him or anyone else after you left. I guess I never really considered us...over. Silly, huh?"

A smile curled one side of Nico's mouth. "I guess we'll just have to be ridiculous together because I felt the same way. And when I told you no other woman would ever know what it was like to be in my bed, I meant it."

"Hurry up and get *this* woman in your bed."

When Nico placed Gadiya down and pulled away, he dragged a finger across the wet spot she'd left behind on his shirt. "You really are ready for me, huh?"

"Ready, willing, and able...to satisfy."

115

"Oh, I have no doubt."

Nico wasted no time undressing. A wave of excitement rushed through her when he removed the fitted black boxers he wore. Licking her lips, she hummed, "Mmm."

Just as she remembered, thick and long.

Nico fisted himself and pumped his hand up and down slowly. "Is this what you want?"

Gadiya gnawed at the corner of her lip, never pulling her eyes off of Nico's impressive erection. "Yes, yes, yes."

Nico climbed into bed and took his place between her spread legs. To her dismay, he didn't enter her. Instead, he kissed her—her chin, her lips, the tip of her nose. Though eager for him to fill her, she cherished his gentleness. He'd always been that way with her. Patient.

Close to her ear, he whispered, "I won't fuck up this time, Gadi bear. I promise." He kissed the tender spot below her lobe. "I promise."

Inching down her body, he captured a hardened nipple between his lips and sucked. The intense sensation made Gadiya squirm with pleasure. Kissing his way to the opposite breast, he flicked his tongue against her nipple in quick succession. The tingle shot through her like a missile and heighten the already potent throbbing between her legs.

Venturing further down her torso, Nico placed a single kiss to her stomach. This time when his tongue touched her clit, it was with gentle, unhurried movement, circling and sucking her...sucking and circling. Stiffening his tongue, he probed her opening, delving in and out.

Gadiya cried out, the orgasm—just as powerful as the first—tore through her like a category five tornado. She held Nico's head in place as he continued to skillfully feast on her. By the time he ended his delicious torture, she was shaking. Still, she wanted more. "I...I need to feel you inside of me, Nico. I've waited long enough."

"Yes, you have." He kissed his way back to her mouth. Against her lips, he said, "Do you trust me, baby?"

"With my life," she said without hesitation.

As they kissed slowly, intimately, Nico inched inside of her just as tenderly. Gadiya's mouth captured his moans, and his captured hers. Eager hands explored Nico's strong, sweat-slickened back and squeezed his tight ass as his unhurried strokes made the room spin. Breathing was like pulling cement through a straw, and every delicate part of her pulsed.

Nico buried his head in the crook of her neck. "Woman, you're going to make me lose my mind. You feel so good. Too damn good."

"I've missed you so much, Nico."

He met her gaze. A lazy smile played on his lips. "You'll never have to miss me again. I'm never letting you go. Ever."

Nico adjusted her legs and drove himself even deeper inside her. She screamed his name.

"Hell, yeah. Scream my name again, baby. It does something to me."

"*Nico...Nico...Nico...*" With each cry of his name, his stroke grew stronger, faster. Gadiya's head arched off the pillow, the warm sensation of an impending release blossoming in her stomach. "I'm coming, Nico." She dug her nails into his flesh, holding her breath, releasing it in a half-yelp, half-shriek when the orgasm struck her head-on.

Blood *whooshed* in Gadiya's ears, but she didn't want Nico to stop giving it to her like a champion. His rhythm grew clumsy, and she knew it signaled him reaching his own climax.

"Hold on, baby," he said, placing his hands behind her knees and pinning her legs to her chest and driving wildly in and out of her.

Gadiya sang out her delight. Each stroke he delivered was more tantalizing than the last. A guttural sound rumbled in his throat. A beat later, he throbbed inside of her, the pulsing intensifying the lightning bolts of pleasure already sparking through her.

"Don't stop, Nico. Not until you've given me every drop."

He seemed determined to do just that.

Eventually, Nico's lumbering strokes came to a gradual end. His chest heaved as his body lowered to her chest. Holding him in her arms felt just as good as the—well, the words *several orgasms he'd brought her to* came to mind, but that would have been a lie.

However, the warmth of his body pressed against

hers was beautiful and something she hadn't realized how much she'd missed until now. When Nico made a move to roll off of her, she protested, "No, not yet."

Nico's head rose to eye her. He brushed a damp hair from her face, and without warning, she burst into tears. A look of terror spread across his face, and she felt stupid for not being able to keep her emotions in check.

"What's wrong? Please don't say you regret being with me."

"Absolutely not," she said through tears.

A look of relief filled his eyes. He wiped her tears away. "Then what?"

"I don't know, but I promise you it's nothing bad."

Nico rolled off of her and onto his back, pulling her into his chest. Securing her in his arms, he kissed her forehead. "As long as they aren't sad tears we're good."

Gadiya rested her head on Nico's chest and listened to the drum of his heart. "I never imagined we'd ever be here again, Nico. Actually, I've imagined it, but never truly thought it would happen."

"Some things are just meant to be, Gadi. I believe that now more than ever. We never should have been apart. I never should have run from the one person who I knew would have been my rock, who I knew could have helped me through. I should have told you what I was going through, baby, the bad memories Phoenix's death brought back. I should have told you everything."

Gadiya pushed up on her elbow and stared into Nico's sad face. "Tell me now."

Nico's eyes slid away, his demons obviously still torturing him. He needed to know he wasn't alone, that she had demons terrorizing her, too. "I haven't visited Phoenix's grave since his funeral."

Nico's puzzled gaze met hers again. With furrowed brow, he said, "Why?"

"I can't. I've gotten to the gates of the cemetery but can't bring myself to enter. I used to visit my mom's gravesite all the time, but now I can't even..." She lowered back to his chest.

"We all have something we can't bring ourselves to do." Nico went quiet for a moment. "My mother killed herself. My mother killed herself," he repeated. His voice cracked. "And I'm the reason why."

Urgently, Gadiya pushed up on her elbow again. "You're not the reason—"

"I am."

Nico's eyes glistened, and she could tell he was fighting back tears. He'd never been one to show much emotion, so she knew he was hurting. It tore her up inside to see him in so much pain. "Tell me," she said in a low, compassionate tone.

Nico eyed the ceiling. "I caught my father with another woman, and I told mother. That's why she took her life." He scrubbed a hand down his face. "If it hadn't been for me and my big mouth, Gadiya, my mom would still be—"

Gadiya pressed her lips to his before any more words could escape. Pulling away, she said, "Don't you dare say it. If you say it, I'm getting out of this bed and leaving." Her words were firm and obviously effective, because Nico remained silent.

"I get it. You need to blame someone, so you blame yourself. I played the blame game with Phoenix's death. It wasn't until Rana made me see that we have absolutely no control of other people or their actions. When I finally accepted that, I felt...free. I believe that freedom helped lead me back to you. Let me help you find your freedom."

Nico pinned Gadiya to the bed and kissed her with so much vigor, so much passion, she swore he would swallow her whole. When he finally pulled away, her lips throbbed, but the pain was worth it. He stared down at her. Though he flashed a flimsy smile, she knew his pain and sadness still lingered just below the surface.

"I'm a lucky man." He pecked her gently. "And for the record, you're not going anywhere. In fact, I'm not sure I'm ever letting you out of my bed."

Allowing him to divert from a clearly still raw subject, she said, "Chief Dupree, are you alluding to kidnapping me?"

"Well, if you want to get technical. I'm sure no one knows you're here."

And he was right. "Your neighbors will remember seeing my car."

"Good point. Well, in that case... Since I can't kidnap you, I guess I'll just have to make you not want to leave."

"Sounds like that could be a whole lot of fun for

one or both of us."

"Oh, you can bet your sweet ass it will be a thrill for us both." Something in his expression changed, grew stern. He searched her eyes. "In the process of you helping me find my freedom, I hope you discover that you still love me."

Too late. She'd already discovered that. But for now, she chose to keep it to herself.

12

Gadiya cursed when she knocked the container of pipe cleaners off the side of her work table. A hundred red, yellow, blue, green, and white fiber covered wires littered the floor. She tossed her hands into the air. Could one more thing go wrong? She sure could use a hug right about now. Where were Nico's arms when she needed them?

When the shop phone rang, she snatched it up. Remembering her pleasant voice, she said, "Good morning, The Twisted Balloon. Gadiya speaking."

"Do you have any idea how bad I want you right now?"

At the sound of Nico's voice, her mood instantly improved. Moving from the back workshop and into her office, she closed the door for a little privacy. "Nico Dupree, you're supposed to be conquering my heart, but every time I turn around, you're trying to conquer my body. What's up with that?"

"I'm a big boy, and big boys have big appetites. And just so we're clear, I have your heart already. It's just a matter of your confessing it. But I'm not rushing you; I'm very much enjoying the conquering. Plus, I want you to be one hundred and ten percent sure. Forever requires that."

"Forever, huh?"

"Did you think I was going for just temporary?"

No, she didn't. He'd made that perfectly clear. He was definitely playing for keeps. Their time together had been magical, like they hadn't spent one single day apart. Before she could respond, there was a knock at her door. "Hold on a second."

The second Gadiya swung the door open, a red-faced, frantic Daniela started babbling. Her hands moved up and down as if she were patting down cotton. Balloons and order mix-up was all that Gadiya caught. Out of all of her interns, Daniela was the most...passionate.

"Slow down, Daniela. I can't understand you."

Daniela pushed her black-framed glasses further up her thin nose, inhaled, then released it slowly. "The balloon manufacturer phoned to say they'd experienced some computers issues and that some orders were incorrectly processed. *Our order*. Our order for the Fireman's Day celebration."

Oh, boy. Gadiya needed this event to go off without a hitch. The reputation of her shop depended on it. "We won't panic, Daniela." *Yet.* She held up an index finger. Lifting the phone back to her ear, she said, "Nico, can I call you back? I'm dealing with an issue here."

"Is everything okay?" Nico asked.

"I sure hope so."

"Call me if you need me."

Gadiya wanted to say I always need you but refrained with Daniela standing in front of her. "Will do."

Clicking the phone off, she returned her full attention to Daniela. "Okay, what exactly did he say?"

Daniela pulled at one of her red locks. "He said not to panic."

This obviously for Daniela was code for panic, because the woman was doing a mighty fine job of it.

"He said our order went to China, and China's order is coming here. He said there shouldn't be a problem getting our order to us. He just wanted to make us aware so that we can refuse the shipment."

Gadiya plastered a smile on her face. "See, everything is fine. No worries."

"You're right. Everything is fine. I get a little anxious sometimes." She blew out a heavy breath, then smiled. "You are so good under pressure, Gadiya. I should get back to work." Daniela turned and sauntered away.

Gadiya laughed to herself. She wasn't as good under pressure as Daniela believed. She'd just perfected faking it. Though she had to admit, a few months ago, she'd been just as spastic as Daniela. But since Nico had come back into her life, she found herself rarely sweating the small things.

The more she thought about it, she liked this new carefree feeling and especially loved the man who'd prompted the change, especially since change wasn't one of her strong suits.

As always, Rana had been right about her finding her happy with Nico. Gadiya hadn't been this happy in a long, long time. Many more blissful days lie in her future. At least one more for sure. Her thoughts shifted to the outing Nico had planned for them the upcoming weekend. The one he'd been extremely tightlipped about.

What did he have in store?

The more she thought about it, it didn't matter. They'd be together, which was enough for her.

By the time Saturday rolled around, Gadiya was teeming with excitement. All week, she'd pondered what thrilling adventure Nico had planned for them. Never in a million years would she have guessed he'd bring her to the Mount Pleasance Cemetery.

Gadiya stared at the black, wrought-iron gates, then shifted her focus to the letters scrolled in gold and studied them again, just in case she'd read it wrong the first time. Nope, they still read MOUNT PLEASANCE CEMETERY.

"How could you bring me here? You know—"

Nico captured her hand in his and kissed the back. "You can do this, Gadiya. You're stronger than you know. I'll be with you every step of the way. But if you're not ready, I won't push."

Gadiya snatched her hand away from him. "I'm not ready. Let's go." Her words were terse and firm.

Though protest danced behind his frown, he didn't attempt to sway her. What was she so afraid of? Why did this place frighten her so much? Nico cranked the engine, but before he could shift into drive, she touched his arms. Without having to say a word, he killed the engine.

When Nico rounded the vehicle to open her door, Gadiya took a deep breath before stepping out. Glancing into Nico's caring eyes, she found strength. "I can do this."

"I know you can."

Gadiya told herself she'd be strong, but the second she stood at Phoenix's grave, she broke down in tears. Like lightning, Nico was by her side. His protective arms held her tight, his hand gliding up and down her back. Man, she hadn't expected such an overflow of emotions.

Nico kissed her forehead. "Do you want to leave?"

"No. I need to do this."

Nico smiled down at her and dried her tears. "I'll give you some privacy."

Though she didn't really want him to leave her side, she nodded. Some things a girl had to do alone.

"I'll be right over there if you need me." He head-pointed to a bench several feet away. Cradling her face, he said, "Only two long strides away."

"I'll be okay."

Nico eyed her for a moment, then slowly backed away as if he dreaded leaving her alone.

On her knees, Gadiya studied the words engraved into the stone. "I've given so many reasons why I haven't visited you, Phoenix. So many excuses." She dragged her hand across her cheek. "But the truth is I was ashamed to come. I blamed myself for your death, thinking if I'd just paid more attention, then maybe..." She sighed. "I blamed myself, but I don't anymore."

Gadiya sat in silence a moment, recalling the last time she'd seen her brother alive. The memory brought a smile to her face. A warm breeze blew across her face, and she closed her eyes, choosing to believe it was Phoenix reaching out.

Opening her eyes, she said, "Things went so dark for me after you died." She shot a glance in Nico's direction. "But things are much brighter now." Gadiya rested a hand on the headstone. "I miss you so much, brother. Every single day. I love you and I always will. You will always live in my heart. Always."

A beat or two later, a cardinal landed so close to her hand, its feathers tickled her fingers.

"Gadiya, watch out."

Nico sprinted toward her, his arms flailing. "Shoo, bird."

By the way he was acting, someone would have thought a pterodactyl was about to swoop down, snatch her up, and fly away. "Nico, what's wrong with you?"

"The last time I was here this same bird—at least it looks like the same bird—tried to attack me."

Gadiya eyed the docile creature. It seemed unaffected by Nico's wild behavior. "I don't think it means us any harm. They say when a cardinal appears, someone from heaven is visiting, letting us know they'll always be with us."

Just then a second bird arrived, fluttering around Nico as if something about him attracted it. Though Nico didn't say anything, Gadiya saw it in his eyes, in the

128

tender expression on his face. He sensed his mother.

Then just like that, the birds were both gone.

"*Wow*." Nico scrubbed a hand over his head, his eyes pinned in the direction the birds had flown. "*Wow*."

"I love you, Nico." It was the first time she'd said the words aloud since they'd gotten back together. "I love you in an intense kind of way that—"

Before she could finish her thought, Nico's mouth smashed against hers. The kiss could have definitely been labeled mildly inappropriate, considering their current setting, but that wasn't enough to break their connection.

That happened when the cardinals returned, joined by a third bird. A blue jay. Instantly, Gadiya knew this one represented her father. He'd been a birdwatcher. Blue jays had been his favorite. Happy tears spilled from her eyes.

Gadiya and Nico watched in amazement as all three lapped circles around them, serenading them with loud, beautiful melodies. Laughter filled the otherwise tranquil cemetery as they both found obvious delight in the actions.

Several minutes more and the birds were gone again, leaving behind love, peace, and happiness.

13

If Gadiya had to sum up her part in the Fireman's Day celebration in two words, they would be *huge success*. She and her crew had totally rocked it. The life-sized burning building, fireman with a hose, and fire engine made wholly of balloons had garnered endless praise.

But it wasn't all of the accolades that had put a colossal grin on her face, that had been a result of the children who'd lit with joy during the face painting, balloon sculpting, and the other activities that had kept them busy all day.

At almost nine in the evening, things in Kiddie Korner had slowed to a crawl. Close to bedtime, she assumed. Though with all of the cotton candy, candy apples, caramel corn, and cider they'd distributed, parents would have one heck of a time getting their little ones to close their eyes.

"Hey, good-looking."

Gadiya beamed at the sound of Nico's voice behind her. When she turned, her lips curved even deeper at the sight of him in the crisp white, long-sleeved shirt. On one shoulder was an American flag patch, the other a MPFD. There were pins on the points of his collar. His name badge was placed on the right side of his shirt, while a shiny gold badge claimed the left. A black tie, black pants, spit-shined black shoes, and a black and gold hat—which he carried under his arm—completed his attire.

"My, my. Don't you look all official?"

Nico took a step back and opened his arms. "You like?"

"Me likey a lot." She straightened his tie clip, then gave him a peck on the cheek. She preferred a long, deep, spine-twisting lip-lock, but didn't want to cause a scene.

"Can I steal you away from kiddie land for a bit?"

"Kiddie Korner," she corrected. "And yes, you can, because this is a celebration for you and your men. So that means, tonight, you can have anything you want."

A roguish smile spread across his face. "Really?"

"Mind out of the gutter, fella."

Close to her ear, he whispered. "Oh, if you only knew."

Gadiya threaded her arm through Nico's, and they strolled arm in arm. By Nico's side she felt like a celebrity. Everyone greeted them as they passed by. It wasn't any secret that they were a couple, but still, it felt kind of awkward for so many eyes to be on them.

"Wow. You're quite popular, Chief Dupree."

"Actually, balloon artist Lassiter, I think you're the cause of all of this attention. That fire scene made entirely of balloons is on everyone's lips. I'm sure the council will agree that your services were money well spent."

Yeah, she had pulled off an amazing feat, considering the balloon mix up that had been quoted as a *no need to worry situation* had turned into a nail-biting ordeal that had thankfully worked out in her favor. "And would my secret benefactor feel the same? Seeing how you footed a good portion of the bill."

Nico stopped and eyed her. "How did—?"

"I know people."

"Are you pissed?"

"Heck, no. I'm appreciative. Especially since at the time, I'd treated you like shit and definitely didn't deserve your kindness."

"Woman, you'll always deserve my kindness. You'll always deserve everything good about me."

He captured her mouth in a heady kiss. *Not wanting to make a scene* went out the window the second their lips touched. There was something about his mouth that beckoned prolonged and passionate. Something that scrambled her brain and banished rational thinking. And she liked it all.

"Fireman and balloon lady sitting in a tree... I bet you gon' need a ladder to get out that tree."

Nico and Gadiya laughed against each other's mouth. Only one person addressed them that way. Greenville.

Greenville was a Mount Pleasant staple. When he'd arrived in town a year ago, he'd told anyone who'd asked that his name was Greenville and nothing else. It was obvious something was a little off with him, but he'd never caused any trouble, so most folks had simply let him be. On occasion, she'd give him small jobs around her shop and paid him in a bounty of food and clean clothes since he'd claimed to have no use for money.

Turning, Gadiya smiled. "Hey, Greenville."

"What's up, Greenville?" Nico said. "Are you still mad at—?"

"*Shhh*," Greenville said, pinning his eyes closed and covering his ears.

"Well, I'll take that as a yes," Nico mumbled.

Somehow Greenville had found out Nico was the one responsible for having the old cardboard plant—Greenville's home—boarded up. For Greenville, Nico usually got the silent treatment, or a tongue stuck out at him. Sometimes both.

Greenville adjusted the purple balloon crown she'd made for him earlier. "Hey, balloon lady," he said, ignoring Nico. "I ate all my popcorn. I'm saving my candy apple for a midnight snack."

Greenville smiled, revealing several missing teeth and a mouth full of decay. He tugged on the dingy green and brown camouflage jacket he wore.

"Where are you staying now, Greenville? Maybe I can bring you something by." Now that the cardboard plant had been boarded up, she wasn't sure where he laid his head. He'd refused to go to the church, which doubled as the shelter for the handful of homeless that called Mount Pleasance home.

"Greenville is a rolling stone," he said. He jabbed a finger at Nico. "You can't hold me down." Then he scurried off.

Gadiya shifted toward Nico. "Did you really have to board up the cardboard plant?"

Something tender flashed in Nico's eyes. "Baby, trust me. If that place caught fire with Greenville or any of his friends inside, it would be a deathtrap. I've been working with the council to come up with a solution for the homeless, especially since the temperature is dropping, but it takes time. Look how long it took for your contract to be approved."

Gadiya wrapped her arms around Nico. "You have a heart of pure gold. Have I told you lately just how much I love you?"

Nico flashed a calculated expression. "No…I…I don't think so."

Though she'd told him several times that day, she said, "In that case, Chief Dupree, I love me some you."

"And I love me some you, too. More than anything on this planet. And I want to spend the rest of my life loving you. Which is why…"

Nico held her at arm's length. When he dropped to one knee, Gadiya froze, the smile sliding from her face. He pulled a red box from his pocket, flipped the top, and presented the most gorgeous diamond ring she'd ever seen.

Her eyes darted around the growing crowd. In a muted tone, she said, "What are you doing, Nico?"

"What I should have done a long, long time ago. I love you with every fiber of my being, woman. I want to spend my life with you." He inhaled and exhaled deeply. "Gadiya Lassiter, will you marry me?"

Gadiya stared wide-eyed at the man she loved more than anything on this earth, then her attention moved to the sparkling diamond. Had she ever seen anything so beautiful? Her heart pounded against her ribcage, and her breathing grew unsteady. The crisp breeze turned into a sizzling inferno and her brain to mush.

"Um...Gadi, baby?"

Her eyes darted to Nico. The expression on his face was a mix of elation and concern. "I...I..."

A second later, she backed away and took off across the square. Gasps sounded around her. She didn't have to be a mind reader to know every woman who'd witness the proposal thought she was crazy for not screaming a resounding yes. And maybe she was, but—

"Gadiya! Gadiya, stop!"

After several more strides, she followed Nico's command. She tightened her hands into fists to subdue the shaking. Her chest heaved up and down from the trek across the square and the anxiousness she experienced from Nico's proposal.

She whipped around to face him. "Why would you do that to me? Why would you put me on the spot like that, Nico?"

"Put you..." He barked a laugh, then his expression turned stern. "Woman, I just proposed to you in front of the entire town and you took off like a ravenous pack of wolves was chasing you."

Gadiya removed the bite from her tone. "Why, Nico? We're doing well like we are."

"Why not, Gadiya? I don't want to just do well

with you, Gadi. I want to do amazing." He took a step closer to her. "Baby, I love you. Do you hear what I'm saying to you?"

She nodded, though she was almost sure the question was rhetorical.

"I love you, and I want to spend the rest of my life with you."

Gadiya cradled herself in her arms. "But you know how I feel about marriage. I thought you were okay with that."

Nico remained composed. "Ten years ago, I was." He shook his head. "But I'm not anymore. I want more, Gadiya. I want to be your husband. What is the issue, baby? Do you not want to spend forever with me, too?"

"You know I do. You know I do," she repeated. "But why do we need a piece of worthless paper to laminate forever?"

Nico clapped his hands together, then rested them against his mouth as if he were attempting to gather his thoughts or to keep from lashing out. A beat later, he continued, "I want you to have my last name, Gadiya. I want our kids to have my last name. I want to be able to introduce you as Mrs. Nico Marshall Dupree."

Gadiya swallowed the painful lump in her throat. Here she stood with a man whom she knew loved her true and unconditional and wanted to spend forever with her. A man who'd stood before the town and asked her to be his wife. A man who was clearly trying his best to understand her hesitation.

"I saw that spark of excitement in your eyes when

I asked you to marry me, Gadiya. What's holding you back?"

"Nico, can't you just accept my answer?"

"No," he said without hesitation. "I want—"

"*I, I, I*. So, it's all about what *you* want?"

"Don't make me the bad guy here, Gadi."

"But it's okay for you to make me one?"

"Do you love me, Gadiya? Truly love me?"

The question took her by surprise. "Do I love you?" Her eyes narrowed on him. "How could you ask me that, Nico? Of course I love you." Why in the hell did he think she was breaking her own heart? She was sparing him. Why couldn't he see that?

Nico stood toe-to-toe with Gadiya and cradled her face in his hands. "There's nothing in this world I wouldn't give you, Gadiya Lassiter, including my last breath. Marry me."

A single tear slid from her eye. "I…" Instead of can't slipping past her lips, she said, "I'll think about it." It was all she could offer at the moment.

Nico's jaw clenched. Relaxing, he took a step back and leveled her with a hard stare. "You'll think about it?"

Exhausted, she said, "What do you want from me, Nico?"

"Obviously…" He turned away briefly. "Obviously, more than you're willing to give."

"Then maybe you should find someone who can give you exactly what you want." When Nico looked at her as if she'd wounded his soul, she felt horrible. *Shit*.

"Nico...I'm sorry. I didn't—" She reached out to touch him, and he pulled away.

Flashing his palms, he backed away, turned, and was gone.

***

Since the disastrous proposal at the Fireman's Day celebration a few days before, Nico had avoided Gadiya like a bill collector. He slammed a file drawer close. What in the hell did she have against marriage? He could understand if she'd once been in a bad one, but she'd never been married.

And what about her parents? They'd had the perfect marriage. She'd seen firsthand how beautiful marriage could be. Shouldn't that alone motivate her? He abandoned trying to figure out the inner workings of Gadiya's mind.

"Knock, knock."

Nico glanced up to see Ollie at his door. "Come in."

"Hope I'm not disturbing you."

Nico took a seat on the edge of his desk. "You're not. What's on your mind?"

"A couple of us are heading to the grocery store. Any requests?"

"No, I'm good. Thanks for asking, though."

"Yeah, no problem. No problem."

Ollie slid his hands into his pockets, rocked back and forth on his heels, and glanced around the room as if he wanted to say more. "Was there something else,

O?"

"Um...I just want to make sure you're really okay. After what happened in the square, I mean."

Nico imagined he and Gadiya had been the talk of the town. He'd almost expected to read it in the Mount Pleasance Gazette: FIRE CHIEF SCORCHED IN BOTCHED MARRIAGE PROPOSAL. The headline would have been about right.

Nico gave a nonchalant shrug. "You win some, you lose some."

"And you live to fight another day."

He wasn't so sure about that. "Yeah, that's what they say."

A beat of silence played between the two men.

"Davena's pregnant," Ollie blurted. "Eight weeks. I'm going to be a father."

Finally, something beautiful to celebrate. Nico held out his hand. "Congratulations, man. That's fantastic news." Ollie's expression was a mix of uncertainty and terror. To help soothed the man, Nico said, "You'll be a great father. A natural." To be honest, he kind of envied the man.

"Thank you. We had our first baby argument last night."

"Oh, yeah?" Nico could tell Ollie wanted to talk about it. Though he couldn't offer a lot on the baby front, he was a good listener. Or so he'd been told. "I hope it wasn't anything serious."

"Nah. She wants me to quit the department."

Obviously, he and Ollie had two completely

different ideas of serious.

"She thinks it's too dangerous now." Ollie laughed. "I reminded her we are in Mount Pleasant, North Carolina. The worst thing she has to worry about is me burning myself on the grill."

Both men laughed.

Ollie scrubbed a hand over his head. "She cried for two hours straight last night."

Inwardly, Nico laughed at the almost traumatized expression on Ollie's face.

"Seven more months," Ollie said more to himself than Nico, then sighed and waved a hand through the air. "Pregnancy hormones. She'll be okay."

Nico clapped him on the back. "I'm sure everything will be fine." He rounded his desk.

"Would you?"

"Would I what?" Nico said, rummaging through a drawer.

"Before getting this cushiony office job, would you have quit if Gadiya had asked you to? I mean, I know you're going through something now, but before that...would you have quit?"

Nico's gaze rose to meet Ollie's. Give up a job he loved for the woman he absolutely adored... "Yeah. But like you said, we're in Mount Pleasant, North Carolina. It's a whole lot different than being in a big city."

Ollie nodded. "You're right. Well, I won't keep you. You sure you don't want anything?"

"I'm sure."

"Okay." Ollie started for the door, then stopped.

"Chief, I've been around women all of my life. My mother, my grandmother, aunts, five sisters. You learn to read them."

"Maybe you can give me a lesson on them." Because Gadiya had him baffled.

"Lesson number one," Ollie said, "Gadiya didn't say no because she wanted to. There was something more, something deeper was holding her back."

Nico folded his arms across his chest and lost himself in his thoughts. Maybe he knew women—at least, his woman—better than he'd given himself credit for because he had gotten that same feeling...that something had been holding Gadiya back. But what?

"Find out what and maybe you can help her conquer whatever it is." Ollie laughed. "No offense, boss, but you haven't been functioning too properly without her."

Nico's brow bunched. "Not functioning properly?"

Ollie pointed to his chest. "Your shirt's on backward." He barked another laugh and left.

Nico dipped his head and laughed at himself. "Damn."

Ollie was right. He and Gadiya needed to talk. Really talk. That was the only way he'd find out what in the hell was going on. She loved him, he knew this. So what was keeping her from taking the next step?

Instead of bombarding her, he'd give it a few more days. Give them both time to get their thoughts together. In the meantime, maybe he'd pay a visit to Rana. If anyone knew what was going on with Gadiya,

Rana would. But would she tell him?

14

Though Gadiya stared at the television, she wasn't paying attention to the feuding couple on the screen. Her thoughts were where they'd been for the past week. On Nico. They were fighting their own battle. Or more accurately, she was fighting a solo feud.

Swallowing, she forced her lingering tears away. She didn't have the right to cry. This was of her own doing. She'd been the one to push Nico away. Now, she had to live with her actions.

"I've lost him again, Rana. This time for good. He hasn't even called me once." Not that she could blame him.

Rana rubbed a hand across Gadiya's back. "No, you haven't. Nico loves you. He's just hurt, Gadi. Hurt and confused. And, truthfully, so am I. I saw it on your face, baby sis, you wanted to say yes to Nico's proposal. Why didn't you? And don't lie to me."

Gadiya slid her gaze away. "I'm afraid. Terrified, actually. I don't…" Her words trailed off, hesitant to deliver the next string.

"You don't what?" Rana urged.

In a low, cautioned tone, she said, "I don't want to end up like Mom and Dad." When Rana didn't speak, Gadiya assumed she'd upset her sister.

"Go on," Rana finally said.

Gadiya wasn't sure she should, but she did. "At

one point, they were so in love. So in love. Then, everything changed. They started fussing over every little thing. It was like they hated each other."

Rana offered nothing. It wasn't like her to not provide commentary. Gadiya figured her words were hard to hear, but she hadn't said anything that wasn't true.

"I don't want—" She paused when a police car buzzed by, its siren blaring. Starting again, she said, "I don't want that to happen to Nico and me. And what about Sadona and Alec? Something is going on with them. I can hear it in her voice when we talk. I don't want to wake up one day, and Nico and I hate each other."

"So, you'd prefer to wake up without him at all?"

"I don't want that either."

"Oh, sweetie, as your big sister and someone who loves you to pieces, right now I have the urge to tell you exactly what I think you *want* to hear: trials won't come, there'll be no bad days, your life with Nico will be perfect." Rana paused. "But if I told you any of that, Gadi, it wouldn't be me loving you; that would be lying to you."

Rana always dispensed the truth and Gadiya had always respected her for it, even if sometimes the truth hurt.

"Since lying is not my thing, I'll tell you what you *need* to hear. That love *ain't* easy. That love *ain't* always pretty. That love definitely *ain't* perfect."

For the first time in a week, Gadiya laughed. In her

head, Gadiya could hear their mother voice, scolding Rana for poor English. Punishment of having a school teacher for a mother. Gadiya wasn't sure who'd gotten chastised more, she or Rana.

Rana hooked her arm through Gadiya's. "Don't sacrifice the love of your life because you believe losing him is easier. Love is messy. Love is hard. Love is demanding. But despite all of that, with the right person, love is so worth the changes it puts us through, so worth the sacrifices we make for it."

Gadiya leaned back onto the cushion. "But Mom and Dad—"

Rana flashed her palm. "You can't compare your and Nico's relationship to Mom and Dad's." She sighed. "Yes, Mom and Dad argued. Sometimes a lot. They disagreed. They nagged each other. They seemed more unhappy than happy at times. But you know the one thing they never did?"

"What?"

"They *never* gave up on each other. Despite all of their trials, they never gave up on each other. That's love, Gadiya. Love in its purest form. It wasn't always pretty, but it was for damn sure real."

Gadiya had never considered the fact that through all of their parent's arguing, they'd always been there for one another. She replayed scenes in her head. When their Dad stormed out, he'd always come back with flowers for their mother. When their Mom had sparked an argument before their Dad left for work, he'd always come home to a feast fit for a king. How could she have not remembered any of this until now?

Rana started to talk again, forcing Gadiya back to reality.

"Don't let doubt dictate your happiness. You're a Lassiter woman. You come from a long line of strong, proud woman. Look that doubt directly in its beady eyes and scream, fuck you!"

Gadiya hollered with laughter and Rana joined in.

Once they calmed, Rana threaded her fingers through Gadiya's. "People aren't perfect. Life's not perfect. Love is definitely not perfect. But when you combine all three—life with the person you love—perfect doesn't matter. Only real matters. And trust me when I say it, Nico's love for you is as real as it gets."

Gadiya rested her head on Rana's shoulder. She'd heard every word her sister had said, and valued them. Still, it would take more than a conversation to change her mind about marriage. But she did appreciate Rana's efforts. "As always, thank you for your prudent counsel. When did you become so damn wise?"

"*Become*? *Hmmph*. Girl, I was born this way."

Their laughter was interrupted by the sound of more sirens.

Rana pushed from the couch and peered through the blinds. "What the… There's smoke. A lot of it. It's coming from the direction of the old cardboard plant."

Gadiya bolted from the couch and hurried to the window. Just as she did, a fire truck zipped by. Instantly, she got that feeling. The one she got every time she knew something bad was about to happen.

***

Nico came to a screeching halt, slammed his truck into park, and bolted out. He was glad he'd stored bunker gear in his truck. Just in case, he'd told himself. Though firefighting was no longer officially a part of his job description, he stayed prepared.

Removing his wear, he suited up just in case his men needed him. He trusted them to get the job done, but this fire could require all hands on deck.

The intense blaze lit the night sky. This inferno would be a headache to fight in the daylight; it was going to be hell fighting it with nothing more than the full moon and licking flames providing the only illumination they had.

Nico raced across the asphalt lot toward where his men were gathered. Clearly exhausted and overheated, several leaned against the engine, while others stood bent at the waist trying to catch a breath.

"Who's inside?" Nico yelled over the roar.

Ray, one of the part-time men, responded, "Brill, Chester, Tank, Morgan, and Ollie."

With the mention of Ollie, Nico looked toward the blocked off crowd, instantly spotting Davena. Even from this distance, he could see the distraught expression on her face. Ray spoke again, and Nico slid his attention back to the man.

"It's hot as hell in there. Low visibility. It's bad, Chief. Real bad," Ray said.

When Ray bent at the waist and started to pour a bottle of water over his head, Nico intervened. "Ray, stop!" Ray donned a confused expression. Nico continued, "You're overheated. The heated condition of your body and the cold water could cause your arteries to constrict." Which could lead to death, especially if Ray hadn't consumed enough liquid.

Visibly shaken by the information, Ray tossed the bottle aside.

Nico's concern grew. Not all of his guys had dealt with a fire this massive before. He knew because he'd sat down with each one of them when he'd first arrived. They were all exceptionally trained, but knowing and doing were two totally different beasts when you factored in adrenaline and fear.

Several men exited the burning building, and Nico felt a wave of relief. It was best to just stand back and let this sucker burn. There was no need to put anyone's life in further danger.

Four. Nico scanned the faces of his exhausted men. "Where's Ollie?"

"He was right behind us," Brill said, dropping to the ground.

"Shit." Without wasting any time, Nico threw on his headgear and darted toward the entrance of the burning building.

"Chief! Chief!" someone called out.

Nico didn't break stride. Judging by the crumbling structure, he only had moments to get in and get out. He never underestimated the dangers of running into an engulfed building. He never over-thought it. He simply always did what needed to be done.

Everyone goes home, he reminded himself.

He prayed that would hold true.

It didn't take him long to locate Ollie, down on all fours, clearly too fatigue to make an escape. "I got you, O."

"*Chief*? What...what are you doing here? You've got a cushy desk job now."

Nico helped Ollie to his feet, then draped Ollie's arm around his neck. "Saving your ass. I don't want to be the one who has to deal with Davena if you perished in this fire."

Ollie managed a weak chuckle. "Yeah, she'd whoop your ass."

Nico wrapped an arm around Ollie's waist. "Let's get the hell out of here."

"Sounds like a great idea to me."

They'd taken several steps forward, when a mound of charred debris fell feet in front of them, blocking their exit route.

Damn.

"That's not good," Ollie mumbled.

Nico cut to the right. If they could just get to one of the boarded up windows, he could kick their way out. Another downpour of flaming rubble rained from above, stopping them dead in their tracks.

"Dammit!" Nico said.

They backed up. Nico quickly assessed their situation and came to an immediate conclusion. They were trapped. He couldn't die like this, not without making things right with Gadiya. He couldn't die like this. Not like this.

15

The first person Gadiya sought when she and Rana arrived at the scene was Nico. His truck idled nearby, the door ajar, but he was nowhere in sight. Her heartbeat kicked up several notches, and she tried to ignore the ghastly feeling swirling inside of her.

Gadiya scanned the weary faces of the first responders. "I don't see him, Rana. Where is he?" she said.

"He's okay, Gadi. He's okay. He's the chief. He doesn't go racing into burning buildings anymore, remember?"

"Yeah. Yeah, you're right." Her mouth said the words, so why didn't her heart believe them. She knew Nico. If his men needed him inside, inside was where he'd be. "There's Davena." If anyone knew what was going on, it was her. Gadiya rushed over. "Davena, have you—"

When the woman faced Gadiya, her puffy red eyes, and distraught expression, sent chills up Gadiya's spine. In that moment, Gadiya realized, in addition to Nico, she hadn't seen Ollie either. Something was wrong.

"Wh—" Gadiya's voice cracked. "Where are they?"

Silently, Davena turned back toward the burning building and sobbed. Gadiya gasped, her legs going weak. Rana steadied her unbalanced body.

Gathering herself, Gadiya draped a shaky arm around Davena. "They'll be okay."

A feeling unlike anything Gadiya had ever experienced coursed through her as the building turned to rubble. *A deathtrap* played over and over in her head. It's what Nico had said about the building once. If it ever caught fire, it would be a deathtrap.

Her bottom lip trembled, and beads of sweat laced her forehead. Despite the heat generating from the blaze, she shivered. Rana stood close for comfort.

Gadiya rested her trembling hand over her heart. *He's okay. Nico is okay. He's trained for this*. She wanted to scream, wanted to cry out to Nico, but she held all of her raging emotions in.

"I heard someone say no one could get inside," Davena said. "That means no one can get out either, doesn't it?"

Gadiya swallowed hard, her words trapped by fear. *They'll be okay*.

Gadiya closed her eyes and wished that this was all a dream. Wished that Nico was there, safe in her arms, nuzzling the side of her neck, telling her...telling her he loved her more than anything on this planet. "Please, Nico, come back to me safe and sound," she whispered to herself. "I can't lose you like this."

A loud explosion forced her eyes open just in time to witness the building crumble down onto itself. The sight sucked the air from Gadiya's lungs. She dropped to her knees, her world collapsing right along with the structure.

While Davena wailed a tortured sound that sliced through Gadiya's entire being, Gadiya didn't make a sound, couldn't make a sound. In her head, she screamed at the top of her lungs, but nothing escaped through her opened mouth.

Darkness and despair crept into her soul. She recognized the feeling all too well. She'd experienced it before, after her mother's death, Phoenix's, her father's. Now Nico's.

But the feeling burning through her like lava was different. Darker. More paralyzing. It siphoned everything from her: hope, happiness, the will to go on.

Rana tugged at Gadiya's arms. "I need to get you out of here, sweetie."

Rana's emotion-filled voice filtered through the chaos swirling around Gadiya. Glancing up at her sister, she calmly said, "But this is where I need to be. Here. With Ni— Ni—"

She couldn't say his name.

Why couldn't she say his name?

Gadiya's chest heaved up and down. "I can't... I can't..."

Tears spilled from Rana's eyes. "You're in shock, Gadi. I need to get you home."

"I can't pick out his coffin. I can't choose the perfect suit for him. I can't plan his funeral. I can't do any of that because I'm only his girlfriend, not his wife. I know what he likes, Rana."

"*Shhh. Shhh.*"

Rana knelt and attempted to help her to her feet,

but Gadiya fought her off. "No, no, no. Don't touch me," she yelled, squirming to break free. Then like time coming to a standstill, she stopped and burst into tears. "Why, Rana? Why Nico? Why? Why does this keep happening? Why?"

Rana cradled Gadiya's trembling body. Gliding a hand up and down Gadiya's back, she said, "We'll get through this. Together. We always do. We'll get through it. I promise. Okay?"

Regaining a faint amount of composure, Gadiya nodded her head. Dragging her hand across her runny nose, she mumbled, "Okay. Okay."

A short time later, Rana pulled into Gadiya's driveway. The entire trip to Gadiya's place had been made in silence. She didn't feel like thinking, let alone talking. All she wanted to do was sleep and forget.

Inside, everywhere Gadiya looked tortured her with a memory of Nico.

"Do you want to lie down?" Rana asked, her voice still trembling when she spoke.

Gadiya shook her head. "I can't go in there. Not yet." If this room smothered her with thoughts of Nico, the bedroom would certainly do her in. "I just want to rest." She stretched across the sofa. "I'm so tired."

Rana removed the throw from the back of the chair and draped it over Gadiya. "I'll fix you something to eat."

Even though she wasn't hungry, Gadiya said, "Okay." Truthfully, she needed a few minutes alone.

When Rana disappeared into the kitchen, Gadiya

closed her eyes and tried to drown out everything around her: the still blaring sounds of sirens in the distance, the hiss from her laptop, Rana shuffling pots and pans.

Though she was sure it was only in her head, Gadiya could smell Nico's cologne, then realized it wasn't an illusion; Nico's scent saturated the crocheted throw. Holding it under her nose, she inhaled deeply.

Gadiya could feel Nico there. Could feel his gentle touch against her warm skin. Could hear his infectious laughter. Tears stung her eyes. Covering her ears to block out the squeal of the sirens, she mumbled, "Please, God, help me through this." She pushed harder and harder against her ears as the nuisance seemed to grow louder and louder. Then, just like that, it stopped.

Thank you.

As if summoned, she opened her eyes. Strobing red light flooded through her blinds. "What...?" Pushing from the couch, she moved to the window and peeped out. When she saw the MPFD pickup truck parked by the curve, she stumbled away. Were they there to do an official death notice?

Nico's words played in her head. *You're stronger than you think.* Gadiya took a deep breath and went to the door. Stepping out, she stood on the stairs and prepared to receive the devastating news.

Gadiya closed her eyes to steady her nerves, but when she opened them, she froze. Were her eyes playing tricks on her? Squinting against the dark, she watched as the figure drew closer and closer to her until he was right there.

"Ni...Nico?"

Warm lips pressed against hers. Her mind reeled from what was happening. Was she hallucinating? Rana had said she was in shock. Maybe this was a result. This could all be a dream. If so, she prayed she'd never wake.

Arms held her tight and flush against a solid frame that felt so familiar. Still, she wasn't convinced she wasn't dreaming. She clung to him, afraid to loosen her grip. The kiss was desperate, hungry, possessive. Tongues sparred, surrendered, waged war again.

The kiss felt real.

Nico felt real.

Her need definitely felt real.

But she had to be sure.

Drawing her mouth away, she cradled his soot-covered face between her hands. His skin was warm, and he smelled strongly of smoke. All signs pointed to him not being a figment of her imagination. "Please tell me you're really here."

Before Nico—or the entity—could respond, Rana's frantic voice filled the air.

"Gadiya! Gadiya! Baby sis, where are you?"

Gadiya couldn't force her eyes away from Nico in fear of him vanishing. A beat later, the screen door swung open, and Rana rushed out. Her feet came to a clumsy stop behind them. Then Rana gasped, dropping something that crashed to the porch.

"Do you see him, too?" Gadiya asked.

"I'm really here, baby," Nico said.

Gadiya released a single sob, smoothed a hand down his cheek, and kissed the tip of his nose. "But how? I saw..." She didn't want to recall what she'd witnessed. "How?" No way anyone could have survived that calamity in one piece.

"*Greenville*," Nico said.

Gadiya's brow furrowed. "Greenville?"

Nico nodded. "He appeared out of nowhere like a guardian angel and led us out through an old ventilation shaft seconds before the entire building collapsed. He saved our lives."

Greenville. Gadiya draped her arms around him. "He saved my life, too. I thought you were dead, Nico. My world ended."

"You're not getting rid of me that easily. I love you, woman. I love you more than life itself. I love you deeper than words, Gadiya. And when I thought I would never get the chance to say that to you again..." Nico's voice cracked. Placing his head in the crook of her neck, he said, "I love you. I love you. I love you." He reeled back and stared into her eyes. "I don't need a piece of paper. I just need you. Nothing else. Just you."

But she needed more. "Nico Marshall Dupree, will you marry me?"

"Oh, my God, yes!" Rana said behind them.

Nico's attention slid to an overzealous Rana, then settled back on Gadiya. "Did you just ask me to marry you?"

"I did. And if you say yes, I will love you without

limit. I will cherish every moment we're together. I will honor you as my man every second we're apart. I'll be your best friend, your lover, your queen." Tears rolled down her cheeks, and Nico brushed them away. "I'll be your sunrise, your clear blue sky. I'll be your refuge, your strength, your truth, your valley, and your mountaintop. I'll love you like no woman has ever dared to love a man, Nico. And I'll do all of this because you are worth it. You are sooo worth. And it shouldn't have taken you almost dying for me to realize my soul is intertwined with yours. No matter how rough things may get, I'll never give up on you, Nico. I'll never give up on us. So, Nico Marshall Dupree, I ask you again, will you marry me?"

"That was so beautiful," Rana said, her voice shaky with emotion. "Say yes, please, say yes."

Gadiya shot her meddling sister a glance over the shoulder. "*Shhh*." She faced Nico again. "So, what do you say, Chief Dupree? Will you allow me to make an honest man out of you?" She smiled, but Nico stood stone-faced.

"Is this what you really want, Gadiya? What you truly want?"

"There's only one thing I ever wanted more."

"And what's that?"

"You safe in my arms. And I got it. Life is unpredictable, Nico. Love is unpredictable. But one thing is for sure, I want to spend the rest of my unpredictable life loving you."

Nico placed his hand behind her neck and inched

her face close to his. Against her mouth, he whispered, "Yes," then captured her mouth in another untamed kiss.

"Well, okay, that's my cue to leave," Rana said, escaping back inside.

When the kiss ended after what seemed like a decade, Gadiya stared into Nico's eyes. "Promise me something."

"Anything."

"That you'll never stop kissing me like that."

Nico's mouth curled into a half-smile. "Baby, I'll kiss you like this until my last breath."

"And I will love you until mine."

LOVE NEVER FAILS…

Six months later…

Gadiya eyed herself in the mirror, barely recognizing her
own face. Thanks to her eldest sister Sadona, her
makeup was flawless. Gadiya turned her head to the
left, then the right, eyeing the diamond studs in her
ears. They'd belonged to her mother.

My something old.

A wave of emotions washed over her, and she
blinked rapidly to banish the tears. There would be
enough of them when she stood before Nico in twenty
minutes and vowed her undying love to him. The
thought caused a warm sensation in her stomach.

Nothing had ever felt as right as this, her wedding
day.

A short time later, Rana and Sadona helped Gadiya
into the sleeveless, floor-length sheath lace wedding
gown. When Gadiya turned toward the full-length
mirror, she gasped. "I look…" her words trailed off.

"Absolutely gorgeous," Rana said, fanning her
eyes. "You look absolutely gorgeous."

"I'm not going to cry," said Sadona, resting her
cupped hands against her lips, blinking rapidly. "Okay,
so maybe I am. Just a little."

Gadiya performed a half turn and scrutinized the
back of her dress. "You don't think it being backless is

too much, do you?" she asked neither sister in particular.

"No," Rana and Sadona said in unison.

"Okay," Gadiya said, smoothing a hand down the front of the white material. "Okay."

"Group hug," Rana said.

All three women huddled into a warm embrace.

"I love you guys so much," Gadiya said. "Thank you for always being there for me. Thank you for your love, support, wisdom..." she eyed Sadona, "and sacrifices. So many sacrifices. I am the woman I am today because of the both of you."

Before Rana or Sadona could respond, there was a tap at the door. A second later, Nico's voice poured in.

"Gadi?"

Gadiya hiked her dress and hurried to the door. "Nico? What are you doing here? You can't see me before the ceremony? Is everything okay?" A small amount of concern crept in.

"I just needed to hear your voice," he said.

Gadiya laughed. "Are you sure you're not checking to see if I'd gotten cold feet and run off?"

Nico chuckled. "That, too."

"I promised you the only place I'm running is to you. I love you Nico Dupree, and I plan to spend the rest of my life doing so."

A beat of silence had passed before Nico spoke again. "That's all I needed to hear. I'll meet you at the altar, baby."

A short time later, Gadiya and Nico pledged their

lives and love to one another in a room full of their closest friends and family, then were presented to the world as husband and wife and for the very first time as Mr. and Mrs. Nico and Gadiya Dupree.

THE END

Dear Reader,

I'd first like to say **THANK YOU** so much for your support! Many of you are spreading the word about Joy Avery romances like wildfire, and I'm eternally grateful! My goal is—and will always be—to continue writing beautiful love stories that take you on an emotional and satisfying journey toward happily ever after. I hope you will stay along for the ride.

I hope you've enjoyed reading **NEVER** as much as I enjoyed writing it. Please help me spread the word about Gadiya and Nico by recommending their love story to friends and family, book clubs, social media, and online forums.

Also, I'd like to ask that you please take a moment to leave a review on the site where you purchased this novel. Reviews help!

I love hearing from readers. Feel free to email me at: authorjoyavery@gmail.com

Until next time, **HAPPY READING**!

ABOUT THE AUTHOR

By day, Joy Avery works as a customer service assistant. By night, the North Carolina native travels to imaginary worlds—creating characters whose romantic journeys invariably end happily ever after.

Since she was a young girl growing up in Garner, Joy knew she wanted to write. Stumbling onto romance novels, she discovered her passion for love stories; instantly, she knew these were the type stories she wanted to pen.

Real characters. Real journeys. Real good love is what you'll find in a Joy Avery romance.

Joy is married with one child. When not writing, she enjoys reading, cake decorating, pretending to expertly play the piano, driving her husband insane, and playing with her dog.

Joy is a member of Romance Writers of America and Heart of Carolina Romance Writers.

WHERE YOU CAN FIND ME:

WWW.JOYAVERY.COM
FACEBOOK.COM/AUTHORJOYAVERY
TWITTER.COM/AUTHORJOYAVERY
INSTAGRAM/AUTHORJOYAVERY
PINTEREST.COM/AUTHORJOYAVERY
AUTHORJOYAVERY@GMAIL.COM

Be sure to visit my website to sign up for my
"WINGS OF LOVE" newsletter!